The Window In The Painting

The Dreary Portent

Megon Lashley

Published by Megon Lashley, 2023.

This is a work of fiction. Similarities to real people, places, or events are entirely coincidental.

THE WINDOW IN THE PAINTING

First edition. May 19, 2023.

Copyright © 2023 Megon Lashley.

ISBN: 979-8223074816

Written by Megon Lashley.

Also by Megon Lashley

The Dreary Portent
The Window In The Painting
The Gold Flower Locket

Table of Contents

To my mom, Celest –

For encouraging all my nonsense.

And to my big brother, Will –

For reading me all those spooky stories.

CHAPTER ONE
The Shop

As the shop door glided open with a gentle nudge, a tiny bell rang out through the air. The sound carried deep into the room and seemed to go on for much longer than such a small bell should have been able. The room overflowed with old objects, antiques collected from all over the world, now waiting to find their perfect home. Dust swirled and danced in the sunbeams streaming through the windowpanes.

The gentle glow illuminated several items in the otherwise dimly lit shop. A glass case housed an old barber's razor in a lavish wooden box. A porcelain doll with dark ringlet hair and a black ruffled dress sat grumpily on a high shelf. Perched and pouting, her glassy eyes fixed in place and her tiny arms folded in a huff. And on the farthest side of the room, only visible by the small amount of light beaming off its finely polished surface, was an elaborate gold locket.

A soft sizzle cut through the air as the smell of sulfur filled the room. A candle on the counter ignited, as if someone had struck a match and pressed it to the wick. The flame cast a soft light through the shadows, stopping just short of a slender silhouette standing behind the counter. She stepped closer, illuminated now.

The young woman grabbed hold of the candle and began her way through the shop toward a bookcase on the wall.

She swept a lock of raven hair from her eyes as she walked, the rings on her fingers glinting as her hand rose into view. Her clothes were a thick, inky black. So dark, in fact, they seemed to swallow the candle's light each time it neared them. She reached the shelf and directed her gaze to the dusty tomes.

Each book on the shelf had a name embossed along the spine; intricate letters in gold leaf. She ran her finger lazily across the row until she landed on the one she wanted. The name on the book glistened with a slight sheen as she pulled it toward her candle. *Lana.*

The woman parted her lips and spoke with a soft, inviting tone. "All things in this shop come with a story. Some are happy, some are tragic, and some are poetic." Her eyes flickered briefly to a grandfather clock stood silent in the corner. Its hands frozen in place. A sign in front of it read: *Do Not Set The Time.*

"This story is one of my favorites." She ran her hand across the cover of the book, tracing Lana's name with her finger. "Lana was an old soul who saw the beauty in things abandoned or forgotten by others. She had the unique gift of being able to see things as they once were, rather than simply as they are now."

As she cracked the spine of the book, the soft leather cover made a gentle squeak.

"I quite like Lana. She and I have a lot in common. We both love old things; objects with a story, rich with history... filled with ghosts," the woman smirked. "Though I can't really say how Lana feels about ghosts these days."

The thick pages of the book crinkled at her fingertips as she turned them with a slow, deliberate hand. Notes and pictures filled the tome, like a dusty, ominous scrapbook of someone's life. She stopped and smiled as she reached a particular page, smoothing the parchment with her palm. "Here we are," the woman said softly, and she began to read aloud...

CHAPTER TWO
Lana

Lana was the type of person who loved old things. She wanted everything she owned to have a history... a story of its own. So when she decided to buy a house in the country, that's exactly what she went looking for. Something old. Something with character. Something with a past. And that's what she found.

The house was the centerpiece of a large estate. Cobblestone walls skirted their way around the property, jagged and slightly crumbling in places. Bits of long dead shrubberies were scattered about the large front lawn. The trees that were still alive twisted awkwardly, their gnarled branches like hands reaching out toward the manor. Clearly, the estate had once been very nice, but it seemed to have fallen into disrepair.

"I got it for a song!" Lana announced with a smile that revealed how proud she was of the purchase.

"You overpaid," Shawn replied plainly.

Shawn never seemed to see the beauty of old things the way his sister did.

"It's perfect," Lana smiled, ignoring him. "Wait until you see inside."

The door opened with a light creak; the breeze disturbing the thick layer of dust that coated the house. Lana inhaled deeply. "Do you smell that?"

"Mold?" Shawn suggested.

Lana rolled her eyes. "History. This place is like a museum. Look at all the great stuff the previous owner left behind!"

The foyer spread seamlessly into a large living space. A dusty couch sat across from an ornate fireplace. Lana ran her hand over the moth-eaten cloth of the sofa, bits of fabric peeling away at her touch. A soft buzz filled the air as the lights flickered on, reluctantly.

Shawn, finger still on the switch, watched the room slowly illuminate. "At least the electricity works," he shrugged and walked toward a particularly stubborn wall sconce that refused to come on.

"That's weird," he said, examining the sconce.

"What is?" she asked, still admiring the battered antique furniture in the room.

"This light," Shawn replied, "It looks like all the others, but inside there's no place for a bulb. It's just decorative, I guess."

"Maybe there was a wiring issue on that wall," Lana suggested. "The house is pretty old. I'm just happy we were able to get the power turned on so quickly."

"And that it works," Shawn added.

"That too," she smiled.

"Who's he?" Shawn gestured toward a large portrait over the fireplace. The lights on either side now illuminated the oil painted canvas.

He was a distinguished-looking man in his late sixties. A soft smile graced his face as his piercing eyes stared back at them. A tarnished golden plaque below the painting read: *Percival Winston Marlow III.*

"That was the original owner," Lana explained. "He loved artwork. There are a bunch of paintings that came with the house."

There was nothing particularly unsettling about Mr. Marlow or the portrait; and yet, staring directly into the face of the man who'd lived there a century earlier gave Lana an odd chill. She shivered slightly.

"See, I told you this place was creepy," Shawn accused.

"It's not creepy," Lana argued. "It's... something else." Without being able to explain what she meant by that, she chose to change the subject. "So, how long will you be gone this time?"

"I'm not sure," Shawn answered. "They're sending me out of the country this time to meet with some promoters in Europe. It'll be at least a couple of weeks, maybe three."

Lana let out a small sigh and focused her attention on an old roll-top desk in the corner of the room.

He must have noticed her disappointment. "Oh, don't look so sad. I'll call you twice a week and I'll be back before you know it."

She gave a small shrug. "I know."

"Plus," he added, "I'm not leaving until Friday, which gives you almost a whole week to show me all the weird old garbage you got with this house." He flashed a teasing grin, "Come on, you know you can't wait to show me some old map you found in the attic, a pocket watch fished out of a heating vent... or some ancient jar of preserves you found in the cellar."

Her eyes lit up. "Actually, there is this really cool trunk in one of the upstairs bedrooms. I think you'll love it!"

"That's the spirit," he smiled, "lead the way."

JUST OFF THE LIVING room stood a wide wooden staircase with a wall on one side and an ornate railing on the other. A worn red carpet ran down the center, leading them up to the second-floor hallway. Dingy flowered wallpaper ran the length of the hall on either side, interrupted by several large oak doors.

"This is where the bedrooms are," Lana announced.

Shawn batted several spiderwebs away from his face and hair. "Charming."

The doors were old, but sturdy. Lana pushed one open with a hard shove. She stepped into the cold, dark room and fumbled for a light switch. "Hang on a second. I've only been here once, but I think the light is on this wall."

Her hand finally met the switch. The lights flickered briefly, and Lana let out a loud scream. A woman stood, staring back at her, in the flickering lights. As the bulbs steadied themselves, Lana looked at the doorway to see her brother doubled over in laughter.

"It's just a mirror, Lan," he sputtered through his snorts. "How are you ever going to manage being in this house alone?"

She let out a long sigh and stared at her reflection in the filthy mirror. She wasn't normally so jumpy. Moving to a new house, and knowing she'd be spending weeks alone in it, had her on edge. Shawn always traveled for work and lived with her when he was home, but his trips usually only lasted a couple of days.

"Is this the trunk you were talking about?" Shawn was now on the other side of the room, staring at a massive steamer trunk. The trunk was a dull olive green color and reached nearly to Shawn's shoulders. It had buckles and latches holding it closed. In the center was a small keyhole. "That is actually pretty nice. It's in good condition, too." Shawn looked around the room. "Do we have the key?"

"Maybe," Lana answered, glancing around the room. "You'd think it would be in here somewhere."

Shawn headed toward a nightstand near the bed and began searching through the drawers. Lana spotted a small roll-top desk similar to the one she'd seen downstairs. She rolled the top back, revealing the desk surface and three tiny drawers. Riffling through each one uncovered exactly the sorts of small objects you'd expect. Discarded pen tips, dried up bottles of ink, hastily scribbled notes on faded bits of parchment.

"I think I found it!" Lana exclaimed, pulling a tiny key out from under some old postage stamps.

Shawn stood from his place searching the nightstand and joined her by the trunk. She slid the key into the lock. With a firm twist, they heard the scraping of metal tumblers, followed by the satisfying click of the latch.

A strong, musty smell filled the air as they pulled the trunk open. On one side hung a handful of expensive looking suit jackets. The other side of the trunk held four drawers.

"Wow, these suits are in great condition." Lana held one of the jackets up to Shawn, measuring it to his chest. "What do you think?"

"I'd be the talk of the town in 1910," Shawn laughed. "I guess vintage is in style. It might impress some of the older clients. Most of them kind of hate me because I don't wear a tie." He rolled his eyes.

"You buy festival films for a movie studio. Why would you need a tie?"

Shawn shrugged. "Your guess is as good as mine. I don't even handle contracts or go to meetings. I just screen the movies and tell them which ones to buy."

"What's your boss say about it?"

"Nate said as long as I keep picking winners, I can wear a bathrobe and a top hat for all he cares. Apparently, I have an eye for hidden gems." Shawn smiled. "I guess movies are for me what creepy old houses are for you."

Lana smiled. To others, it seemed like she and Shawn had nothing in common. She loved dingy antiques, wine, and relaxing with an old book. She even owned a vintage clothing shop in town with her best friend, Janey. Shawn, on the other hand, loved new things. He loved travel, art, and angst. His favorite thing was finding a tortured artist and introducing their work to the world. They seemed very different, but they saw the world through the same type of lens. They both saw what was hiding from everyone else. The sparkle of what something could become. And it made each of them great at their jobs.

"You're warming to this place; I can feel it," Lana grinned as she opened one of the trunk drawers. "Oh, wow! These are gorgeous." She lifted her hand and revealed a pair of gold cuff links.

"Nice." Shawn inspected the gold engraving. "Those'll sell fast."

"Do you want me to leave the suits for you?"

"Nah," Shawn took a seat on the bed, "I don't need to impress anybody. Sell them in your shop." Shawn leaned back and yawned. "So, which room in this place is mine?"

"Well, I've got dibs on the room next door. Four-poster bed, huge closet, and this amazing antique sewing machine. But aside from that, you can take whichever one you want."

"How many bedrooms are there?" he asked.

"On this floor, there are four bedrooms and one ridiculously over-sized bathroom."

Shawn raised an eyebrow. "What's an *over-sized* bathroom?"

"You're going to love this." Lana motioned for him to follow her. They walked down the hallway and toward the back of the house. Lana led the way to a sturdy door standing opposite the bedrooms. They pushed the door open and walked inside. Shawn swatted instinctively as a stray piece of spider silk floated into his short, blond hair.

The lights slowly came to life, illuminating the ornate bathroom. The room was alight with a rich verdant glow, decorated in shades of emerald glass that reflected the soft light around the room. Shawn's eyes widened, their normal blue hue replaced with the greenish glow of the room. A fainting couch, a vanity, and a huge claw-foot bathtub took up a small portion of the lavish washroom.

"Can *this* be my room?" he asked.

Lana smiled. "Sorry, but you have to share."

AFTER LOOKING AT EVERY room, Shawn eventually settled on the first one he'd seen. By the time Lana got back upstairs with her bag, he'd already emptied the contents of the steamer trunk and put his own clothes in their place. A hundred-year-old trunk was now filled with leather jackets, band t-shirts, and mismatched socks.

"I put everything for the shop in there," he pointed to a cardboard box on the floor.

"Did you find anything you wanted to keep?" Lana asked.

Shawn shook his head. "Just the trunk."

Lana picked up the box and headed into the hallway.

"Hey, Lan?"

"Yeah?" She looked back.

"I really like this room."

Lana grinned, "I told you this place would grow on you."

"Yeah, yeah, don't gloat." Shawn smiled and pushed his bedroom door closed.

Lana walked into her new room. Exhausted, and knowing that she had a lot more work ahead of her the next day, she tossed herself onto an overstuffed chair near the bookcase. She looked at the clock on the nightstand. It was only nine o'clock, but with the way she felt, it might as well have said four in the morning. Unpacking the rest of her stuff would have to wait.

Settling into bed, Lana closed her eyes and acclimated herself to the sounds of her new home. The thumping of the water heater. The whooshing of the vents. The gentle groaning of the old pipes that weaved themselves through the walls. She could hear Shawn walking up and down the hallway. He was always restless when he was home; she knew he preferred to be traveling. She let the sounds wash over her; each thump in the walls, each creak of the floors, creating their own rhythm.

It didn't take long for those sounds to drift further and further away. And before she'd even had time to worry about all the things she hadn't finished, or obsess about what still needed to be done, Lana was asleep.

CHAPTER THREE
Exploring The House

The house looked nicer in the morning light. Something about the pale orange glow beaming off the brass fixtures and tarnished picture frames gave the kitchen a dreamy glimmer. As Lana sat, sipping her coffee, she heard Shawn's footsteps coming down the stairs.

"I smell food," he said, rounding the corner into the kitchen.

"Good morning to you, too," Lana smiled.

"Morning." Shawn grabbed a plate and piled it with pancakes. "I haven't eaten since lunch yesterday. I'm starving."

"Did you end up getting any sleep last night?"

"Out like a light; must've slept about twelve hours," Shawn laughed, joining her at the breakfast bar. "How 'bout you?"

"Pretty much the same," she lied. The truth was, she'd been up for hours. She'd managed to sort through three closets-worth of old clothing since dawn.

Shawn looked across the house at the boxes stacked in the foyer. "You've been busy. Want me to drop those off with Janey?"

"If you're headed into town, that'd be great."

"Yeah, I've got to pick up some bulbs," he said. "I burned out one in my room last night and this morning I noticed there was one out by the stairs to the attic."

"Wow, you went up to the attic?" Lana asked, surprised. "I thought attics creeped you out?"

"They do. That's why I noticed the light was out. I don't need the light so I can *go up*; I need it so I can see that nothing is *coming down*."

"Awe, is Shawn afraid of ghosts?" she teased.

"Ghosts, monsters, attic demons, take your pick. You can let them have you, but I'll pass," he said, finishing the last of his breakfast.

"Do you really believe in ghosts?" she asked genuinely.

"Believe in them and maintain a healthy respect for them." Shawn walked over to the pile of boxes next to the door. "I'll be back in a few," he said, hefting up two of the heaviest boxes with ease.

It didn't take Shawn long to get the boxes loaded into his car. Lana watched from the window as he drove away. She stared out at the long neglected lawn and imagined the magnificence it once had. While she would have loved to see the yard returned to its former glory, she wasn't keen on being the one to do it. The inside of the house was much more to her taste and expertise. She didn't know anything about plants, or flowers, or making things grow.

In truth, Lana wasn't an outdoorsy soul. She did appreciate a beautiful garden, but you'd be unlikely to catch her strolling through one. Even as a child, she never particularly liked summer. While she enjoyed the time away from school, she preferred to stay inside; hidden in a blanket fort in her room, reading a book; or up in the attic, looking through old boxes for treasures her parents had forgotten. She dreaded when her parents would suggest that she *go outside and play*. The summer sun was hot and overbearing, and it burned her pale eyes and skin. Even now, she could feel her blue eyes beginning to water and redden.

Lana turned away from the window and looked around the living room. She let out a deep sigh. The portrait of Mr. Marlow loomed above her. "Looks like it's just you and me, big guy." He seemed oddly disapproving today. Perhaps he didn't like her selling all his fancy clothes. Or maybe he just didn't care for strangers going through his closets.

She sat herself at the roll-top desk in the living room. Rolling up her sleeves and tying her blond locks into a messy ponytail, she began opening drawers and sorting through their contents. The papers, as far as she could tell, all belonged to Percival Marlow. Old receipts and correspondence, all bearing his name. If anyone had lived in the house since him, there was no evidence of it.

Lana was lost for hours, wrapped up in reading the notes and letters that filled Mr. Marlow's desk. She looked over at a stack of receipts. Construction, landscaping, plumbing; all costs incurred while building the house. Most of them seemed pretty ordinary, but one caught her attention; *sconce latch*.

"Sconce latch? What's a sconce latch?" Beneath it was a drawing of one of the wall lights. It was an odd-looking diagram. The sconce itself seemed normal, but behind it there were all sorts of levers and gears. Lana squinted and tried to read the tiny notes written on the blueprint paper. Most of it seemed like technical jargon she wasn't familiar with, but she did recognize one phrase; *pull to unlatch the locking mechanism.*

As she pressed her face closer to the minuscule writing on the paper, trying to glean any further information, she was interrupted by the sound of the front door opening. She must have been quite a sight when Shawn walked in. Desk drawers, open and askew;

papers all over the floor; and her face scrunched up as she looked over the unusual design in front of her.

"What happened here?" Shawn gestured to the mess of papers strewn everywhere.

"I got a little sidetracked," Lana smiled sheepishly.

"You don't say." Shawn rolled his eyes.

"No, really, it was worth it!" Lana rushed over to him, clutching the diagram. "Check out what I found."

Shawn examined the paper. "It looks like our wall lights."

"Right, except it says it's a latch. Look right there, it says *pull to unlatch*."

Shawn looked closer at the writing. "One of the lights unlocks something?" Both of their eyes darted immediately toward the bulb-less sconce in the living room. "That's why there's no place for a bulb."

Lana smiled, "Because it's not a light."

CHAPTER FOUR
The Sconce

They made their way across the room and stood next to the bulb-less lamp. They glanced at one another, neither daring to say a word. Lana's hands trembled with excitement. Her mind reeled with the possibilities; wall safes, secret stashes, hidden exits. In all her time exploring old houses and buildings, she'd never come across anything like that herself. She took a deep breath and steadied her nerves. Shawn also looked nervous, though she realized it was probably for different reasons. Lana gave him a reassuring smile and nodded.

Shawn reached up and, grabbing hold of the sconce, pulled down hard. The metal gave way with a loud, deep clank. The sound of gears and levers grinding against one another came from within the walls. Lana put her ear to the wall, listening to the whirring and scraping bits of metal. Seemingly against its will, a large piece of the wall slowly slid open, recessing into the panel nearest it.

The newly removed wall revealed a narrow, rickety staircase leading downward.

"Does this place have a basement?" Shawn asked, a crackle in his voice that wasn't normally there.

Lana stared, unmoving, into the black nothingness below. She peered deep into the shadows, trying to force her eyes to see something in the void. An odd hissing, barely audible was emanating upward from the darkness. She listened harder, straining to hear it clearer.

"Lana? Lana!" Shawn shouted for her attention.

"Huh?" she pulled her eyes away from the staircase to look at Shawn.

"Does it have a basement?"

She hesitated and shook her head. "Not that anyone told me."

She looked back at the rotting wooden steps in front of them. There were no lights or switches on the walls, just darkness and the smell of damp. The sound had faded, leaving silence in its place.

"Hang on," Shawn said, disappearing for a moment. He returned holding a large flashlight. He shined it down the stairs. Several of the steps had rotted and fallen away. "Oh, that's bad. Maybe we shouldn't go down there."

He continued to shine the flashlight on the room below. There were some old, deteriorating crates filled with filthy cloth. There were, what looked like, left over construction supplies. And in the back, just behind a pile of bricks and boards, Lana caught sight of the edge of a frame.

"I think there's a painting down there." She tested the first step with her foot to see if it was strong enough to hold her.

"No, no, no. Bad plan," Shawn argued. "That looks dangerous."

"I just want to grab that painting, then I'll be right back. You stay up here and hold the flashlight for me." Something about seeing that painting abandoned in a hidden-away room dissolved any fears she may have had about going down there.

"They hid this room for a reason, Lana." But his pleading fell on deaf ears.

She navigated the decaying steps, springing over the missing boards, until she reached the cold stone floor below. The smell of stale air and mildew was much stronger once she was in the middle of it. She pulled her shirt up over her face, trying not to inhale whatever had been growing down there over the last hundred years. She made her way over to the picture frame and grabbed hold of the edge. Someone wedged the painting behind a small gap in the bricks of the wall. With a quick yank, she dislodged it and made her way back to the staircase.

Lana handed the painting across the gap and up to Shawn. Getting down the stairs had proven easier than getting back up.

"Careful," he warned, "I don't think it's going to hold."

He shined his light on the missing steps. Getting a foothold, she used the railing to hoist herself over the gap and onto the next step. Her foot landed with a crunch as the board she settled on began to crack and splinter. Just as it broke out from underneath her, she felt Shawn grab her arm and pull her up into the house. The sound of the falling boards thudded to the ground below them. Shawn grabbed the sconce and pushed it back into position, closing the hidden door.

"Let's never open that again," he said with a heavy breath.

"SO," SHAWN BEGAN, GRABBING her hand and hoisting her up from the floor, "you want to show me what was worth dying for?"

Lana hadn't looked at the painting yet either. She glanced over and saw it leaning, face to the wall, where Shawn had tossed it so he could rescue her. She pulled the painting away from the wall and looked at it for the first time. Her mouth dropped, her eyes widened slightly.

Shawn looked alarmed. "What's wrong? What is it? If it looks haunted, we can just toss it back down there." He headed back towards the sconce, as if to re-open the hidden door.

Lana smiled, "It's beautiful."

"What?" He stopped and looked back at her.

She turned the painting so he could see. "It's our house."

The painting was an exact copy of the exterior of their new home. It was in near-perfect condition, with only a few scrapes along the frame where Lana had pulled it from its hiding place. It showed no signs of wear or mold, despite being in such terrible conditions for so long.

"That's really nice." Shawn's nerves seemed to have calmed. "Why was it down there?"

Lana examined the painting closer. "Probably because of this." She pointed to the signature in the corner.

"Percival Marlow," Shawn read aloud.

"He must have painted this and then hid it down there."

"Why?" Shawn questioned.

Lana shrugged, "Hard to know. People are their own worst critics. Maybe the proportions were off, or he didn't get some little detail just right. Lots of artists hide their work if they don't like how it turned out."

Shawn looked up at the portrait of Mr. Marlow. "Sorry, Percy, but we like it, so it goes on the wall."

Lana beamed at her brother. "See, worth it."

"Yeah, yeah. Let's find a place to hang this."

CHAPTER FIVE
Seems A Little Haunted

Hours of sorting, searching, and unpacking had taken its toll on Lana. She rose from the floor of a downstairs closet she had been filling with their own belongings. She stretched and let out a soft yawn, stepping out from the closet and into the living room. On her way to the staircase, she passed where Shawn had hung their newly discovered painting; stopping for a moment to admire it before heading to bed. She squinted her eyes and leaned closer to the painting. She studied it for a moment, then turned to go upstairs.

As Lana walked toward her room, she heard a loud pop come from Shawn's open door.

"Not again!" he shouted.

"What happened?" she asked from the doorway.

Shawn pointed at the dark corner of his room, an aggravated expression on his face. "I just replaced that bulb and it's burned out again. What is going on with it?"

Lana had no time to respond.

BAM! BAM! BAM! A loud thumping came from behind one of Shawn's walls. Startled, they both turned toward the wall and stared at the origin of the noise.

"What was that?" Shawn asked.

Lana furrowed her brow. "Probably just pipes."

The noise came again, louder this time and with an odd groaning behind it. *BAM! BAM! BAM!* Over and over, coming from within the wall.

"That was not pipes." Shawn's face was pale. "I'm sleeping downstairs tonight."

"Seriously?" Lana laughed.

"Seriously." He grabbed a pillow and blanket off his bed.

"Yeah, best to be safe," Lana teased. "It might be a spoooooooky ghost."

"Not funny, Lan!" he shouted back as he headed down the hallway and toward the stairs.

Lana stayed behind for a moment, eying the wall suspiciously. Walking closer, she ran her fingers over the surface, little chips of paint flaking off under her nails. "Probably just pipes…" she repeated to herself.

LANA'S ROOM WAS QUIET and still. She lay in her bed, quite certain that Shawn was being silly. She had no problem believing in the supernatural, but if she were going to be afraid of ghosts lurking in every noisy old house, she wouldn't be able to do her job. Most of the items in her shop were from houses like that.

Still, it scared Shawn; and so she resolved to be nicer to him about it. It had never occurred to Lana before that the reason her brother didn't share her interest in history may have been a fear of stirring up more than memories. Though, knowing herself as she did, if an item or house she encountered did turn out to be haunted, she'd probably love it even more.

As thoughts of haunted houses flooded Lana's thoughts, darkness filled her eyes. And she drifted off to sleep.

Lana woke with a start. A loud crash came from Shawn's room. It clattered and banged, echoing through the walls. It sounded as if the whole house was falling down around her. She stumbled out of bed and across her room, eyes still half closed.

"Lana!" Shawn's voice shouted from down the hall. "Lana!" he shouted again. He sounded terrified.

She fumbled with her doorknob and raced into the hallway. The banging and crashing had stopped, but she knew it was coming from the direction of Shawn's room. She reached his door and flung it open, only to be greeted by darkness. Shawn's room was quiet. His bed un-slept in, pillow and blanket still missing.

"Shawn?" she called into the darkness.

No reply.

She ran back into the hall and toward the stairs, floorboards creaking beneath her feet. As careful as she could be in the dimly lit staircase, she made her way down to the main floor. Lana's eyes adjusted to the darkness. She peered through the shadows of the living room. There, on the couch, slept Shawn. He didn't stir or show any sign of distress. In fact, it didn't seem like he'd heard any of the commotion coming from his room above.

She breathed a sigh of relief. He was safe. She didn't know what the noise was, but she was glad it wasn't him.

Lana crept back up the stairs, careful not to wake Shawn. Perhaps the whole thing had been a nightmare. Maybe all the strangeness of the day had bothered her more than she'd realized, setting her imagination wild. She reached the top of the stairs, stopping for just a moment to look at Shawn's door. She sighed again, her body trembling and exhausted, and continued down the corridor. The hallway was aglow with a pale orange light that led her back to the safety of her room. She climbed into the comfort of her blankets and quickly found herself back asleep.

LANA CAME DOWN THE stairs to the smell of breakfast. Shawn stood in the kitchen, plates of bacon, eggs, and French toast on the counter in front of him.

"Wow, you've outdone yourself!" She admired the buffet of foods in front of her. "What's the occasion?"

Shawn shrugged. "I may have overreacted a little last night. It was a weird day. You're right, it was probably just normal house noises."

Lana looked a little sheepish. "Actually, I feel bad about teasing you."

"Really?"

"Those noises *were* pretty weird. And they didn't stop. I woke up in the middle of the night to all kinds of commotion coming from your room. I even thought I heard you in there yelling for me." Lana laughed a little at how absurd that must have sounded, but Shawn looked concerned.

"You heard *me*?"

She shook her head dismissively. "I was half asleep; I don't know what I heard."

Shawn still looked troubled by her story, but he didn't push it any further. "So what's the plan for today?" he asked, changing the subject.

She hesitated. "You're probably not going to like it."

"The attic?" he groaned.

"Sorry. I have to sort through it sometime."

"I know. I just hoped it would be while I was gone."

"You don't have to go up there," she promised. "I just need you to take the boxes to Janey once I've sorted them."

"It's fine, I can help," he said.

At Shawn's insistence, they headed up to the second floor immediately. He wanted to start on the attic as soon as possible, not wanting to still be up there come nightfall. They stopped in the spare room, just before the attic stairs. Lana shoved the door open as hard as she could. The wood of the frame splintered slightly as the door scraped against it.

"This one sticks sometimes," she explained.

The air was mustier than the other rooms of the house and everything seemed less cared for. The furniture was covered in stained and tattered sheets; they were old, too old to have been placed there by the estate agent. It seemed like this room had gone unused even in Mr. Marlow's time. In the corner sat a pile of very new-looking cardboard boxes. They looked out of place amongst the rest of the aging decor. Lana had been using this room for storage, since neither she nor Shawn had any use for it.

They each filled their arms with empty cardboard boxes and headed down the hall. The sconce next to the attic staircase flickered mockingly as Shawn passed. He eyed it for a moment, but kept walking. As they headed up, Lana found the switch on the wall that lit the way. The lights weren't very bright, but they were enough to guide them upward toward the attic door.

CHAPTER SIX
The Attic

The attic was large and open. Light shone in from a window at the end of the room. Wooden crates were stacked on top of one another, affixed with paper labels, but any writing had long since worn away. Through a thick mess of spiderwebs, Lana could make out the shape of a wardrobe on the far wall.

Shawn used a tool from a nearby shelf to pry open one of the crates. The lid gave with a loud cracking sound. He waved a cloud of dust away from his face and let out a small cough.

Shawn peered into the crate. "Oh, that's normal," his voice brimming with sarcasm.

"What?"

He reached into the box, pulling out a wooden clown doll. "Box of clowns." He reached in with his other hand, revealing another clown. Shawn gave the clown a sideways look. "That's a normal, sane, non-serial killer kind of thing to have in your attic."

Lana peeked into the box. "There are dozens of them."

Shawn nodded and raised his eyebrows. "We're off to quite a start. Can't wait to see what's in the rest of these."

Sweeping webs and debris out of her path, Lana headed toward the old wardrobe. She heard another loud crack coming from the crates behind her.

"Puppets," Shawn called out. "Box of puppets this time... am I having a nightmare? Is that what's happening?"

Lana laughed and continued toward the wardrobe.

It was a towering piece of furniture. The wood was a smooth dark cherry, with no rough edges or blemishes on its surface. She reached her hand up to the brass catch holding the door closed. With a soft click of the latch, the doors unlocked. Lana pulled the handles toward her; the hinges were stiff, but eventually they gave in. The doors swung wide, revealing the contents.

Winter coats, scarves, and hats filled the wardrobe. Lana reached down and opened one of the boxes that lined the bottom of the cabinet. A supple leather loafer met her eye. She toppled the lid off of another of the boxes. A perfectly brushed and polished men's dress shoe. Some of the shine had worn after decades hidden away, but Lana could tell how cared for they had been.

She heard another loud crack from the crates behind her, but no word from Shawn about what it contained. She was just about to call back and ask him what he'd found this time, when something caught her eye. Bound in leather and tucked away behind a shoebox was an old journal. Lana pulled the journal from the wardrobe and examined it. Thick letters, pressed deeply into the leather, read: PW Marlow III.

She opened the cover and saw that it was filled with entries; beautiful, inky handwriting covered every page. "My home is finally complete," she read aloud from the first entry. But that was as far as she got. She was interrupted by the sound of music coming from somewhere in the attic behind her. An odd, jagged tune floating through the air. It almost sounded as if it was being wound backward. The music stopped abruptly with a loud pop and the sound of a scraping metal spring.

She walked over to the crate to investigate. There was Shawn, sitting on the floor, playing with a toy jack-in-the-box.

He looked up at her innocently. "What? I like this one." Shawn had pushed the doll back into the box and was winding it again. That same unnerving, backward music began to play. The lid burst open as the spring popped out from the box. Shawn held it up for Lana to see. The jester inside wasn't cute or charming, like a normal toy. It had a horrible, twisted face, wide eyes, and a menacing, toothy grin.

"Kinda cool, right?" Shawn smiled.

Lana furrowed her brow and looked on in horror. "Seriously? I thought you were afraid of attic demons. *That's* an attic demon if I've ever seen one!"

Shawn gasped in mock offense and covered the jester's ears.

Lana rolled her eyes.

"I'm keeping this," he announced.

"Keep it in your room," Lana warned. "That thing is nightmare fuel."

Shawn turned his attention to the jester. "Don't listen to her, Mortimer; she's just jealous. She knows she'll never be as cool as you are." He dinged the small bell on the jester's hat with his finger and smiled at the hideous toy.

Lana looked at the other jacks in the crate. A few of them had popped out of their boxes. None of them were as weird or scary as Mortimer. "Why would you, of all people, pick the creepiest one?"

"The scary ones keep the monsters away," he laughed.

She had a sudden flash to their childhood and a tiny Shawn packing around an absolutely grotesque stuffed toy. It was ratty and blood-red, with large patches of fur completely worn away. One eye was missing. Its legs were different lengths. She couldn't even tell what sort of animal it was supposed to be, or if it was an animal at all. Suddenly, his love of Mortimer, the nightmare jester, made sense.

Shawn sat Mortimer on the edge of the puppet crate. "Watch them for me," he instructed the little jack-in-the-box. "Puppets are not to be trusted." And he went to open the next crate.

"You're so weird." Lana shook her head and laughed as she headed back to the wardrobe.

She gathered as much of the winter clothing as would fit in the boxes and took them down to the foyer. It was getting late, so taking them to the shop would have to wait. She passed by the painting of their house. Lana scrunched up her face and pressed it close to the surface. Mr. Marlow had abandoned it for a reason, and the more she looked, the more she realized that there *was* something odd about it. Nothing worth hiding it away in a secret basement, but there was *something*.

She walked back into the attic to find Shawn heaving something large out from behind the crates. He dragged out an enormous wooden sign, hefting it over to the dwindling light of the attic window. "Hey, check this out, Lan!" He showed her the sign. "I guess this explains why the man had thirty-six clowns in a box in his attic."

"*PW Marlow's Toys & Collectibles*," she read aloud. "He must have owned a toy store."

Shawn looked out the window at the fading light of the day. "We should probably call it a day," his voice filled with apprehension.

Lana nodded in agreement and grabbed a box under each arm. Shawn stacked several filled boxes on top of one another, topping the pile with little Mortimer, and hoisted them in the air. Shawn stopped at the spare room and dropped off the boxes, then he and Mortimer disappeared into his room.

"Sleeping in your own room tonight?" Lana called out.

He popped his head back into the hallway. "Giving it a try. After all, it was just pipes, *right?*" he said, sounding completely unconvinced.

Lana smiled. "Right." And she headed into her own room.

CHAPTER SEVEN
Whispers & Windows

Lana lay in her bed, half awake, half dreaming. Wooden clowns danced up and down the hallway. Their tiny footsteps making terrible tapping noises, echoing off the walls of her room.

"Lana," they whispered in their strained voices. "Lana..." they whispered over and over.

Lana woke with a start and sat up in bed. The whispers still lingering in the air. "Lana..." It was faint. It sounded like it was coming from Shawn's room, but it was too faint and hollow to tell if it was Shawn. She heard the squeak of the floorboards in the hallway and the patter of someone's feet.

"I'm still asleep," she reassured herself.

She laid her head back on the pillow and closed her eyes. "I'm still asleep," she repeated. She heard the creaking of the floorboards again. This time, it was moving away from her room and down the hallway toward Shawn's. She crept from her bed and carefully opened her door. The wall lights were all lit, giving a clear view of the corridor and who ever was creeping through their house. But there was no one there. Just the sound. The sound of footsteps and creaking floorboards making their way up and down the hall.

Lana closed her door and raced back to her bed. Breathing heavily, she pulled the covers over her head. "It's just the house settling, it's just the house settling," she panted from beneath the blankets. She slammed her eyes shut and kept them closed tight until the footsteps faded completely.

Lana sat in the quiet of her room. No more whispers. No more pattering of feet. No more sleep. She listened for hours, hearing no stirring from the hallway. Her room began to brighten as dawn peeked through the curtains of her room, casting a pale blue light all around her. She lifted herself from the safety of her bed and tiptoed down the stairs to the living room. The living room was still dark, but the kitchen was showing signs of morning light. She poured a cup of coffee and sat on the arm of the couch, staring at the painting they'd found in the basement.

As the sun shone in through the window, casting its beams softly onto the painted canvas, she furrowed her brow. She stared a moment longer, then stepped closer. Something had been bothering her about the painting, but she hadn't been able to put her finger on what. Now, seeing the light from the window streaming onto its surface, she realized that there was something not quite right.

"Morning."

Lana jumped, still on edge from her lack of sleep. She hadn't even heard Shawn coming down the stairs. "Morning," she recovered.

"Rough night?" He headed to the kitchen and poured himself a coffee.

She sighed. "You could say that." She thought about telling him about the footsteps in the hall, but decided against it. She didn't want him packing his stuff and moving out. "How was your night?" she asked, skirting the conversation away from herself.

"It's out again," he said with a huff.

"What is?"

"The light in my room," he answered, taking a sip of his coffee. "This is the third time."

"Same light every time?"

Shawn nodded. "There must be a short in it. I'll call an electrician to take a look. I'm not feeding that thing anymore light bulbs."

"What about the light by the attic staircase?" Lana asked, remembering he'd changed that one recently as well.

"Thankfully, that one's fine. If that one mysteriously burned out every night, I'd be moving."

Lana took that as further confirmation not to tell Shawn what she'd heard the night before. He'd overreact. It was probably nothing. Just a creaky old house playing tricks on its new owners. Lots of other noises sound like pacing footsteps. She wracked her brain trying to think of even a single example of a noise that might mimic that sound.

"Ready for me to take those boxes of clothes to Janey?" Shawn asked.

Lana nodded. She helped him pack the boxes into his car and watched as he drove down the long gravel driveway toward the road. She looked out at her lawn; dry, dead, and shriveled. Even the weeds had given up and blown away. A gnarled tree shook slightly as an entire flock of black birds fluttered from its branches. They flew all at once in a beautiful cloud of feathers and wings, silhouetted against the sky. Her eyes drifted to a small hill toward the front of the house. Judging by the distance, it was probably where Percival Marlow had sat to paint the artwork of the house.

THE WINDOW IN THE PAINTING

LANA GRABBED THE PAINTING from its place on the living room wall and carried it out to the hill in front of the house. She held it up in front of her. This was exactly where he'd been when he painted it. She kept the canvas up in front of her and carefully looked back and forth from the painting to the real house.

"You," she said, pointing at an upstairs window in the painting. "You're not on the real house."

Lana stared back at her home, examining the place where the window would have been. "Why would he paint it if it weren't there?" A window *must* have been there when he made it. She looked at the window in the painting, then back to her house. "That's Shawn's room." At least as far as she could tell. They'd only lived there a few days and so she couldn't be completely certain. But Shawn's bedroom *was* the first room in the hallway and closest to the front of the house. "Why would Marlow have removed a window?"

She stood, pondering the reasons why a man might remove a window from the home he'd just built, when something caught her attention. In the distance, she saw a truck she didn't recognize pull up to the house. She walked down and greeted the man. He was wearing coveralls and carrying a toolbox.

"Someone call about a light?" the man asked.

"Yeah, the bulbs keep burning out in one of the bedrooms," Lana explained. "I'll show you where it is."

She led the electrician up the stairs and to Shawn's room. She pointed to the faulty wall sconce. Mortimer was sitting on Shawn's trunk, bobbing happily and staring at the man as he entered the room. He eyed Mortimer for a moment as he passed, shook his head, and kept walking toward the light.

As she stood in the doorway, she heard the front door and Shawn's footsteps coming up the stairs. The electrician had all kinds of questions about the light, the house, if there were any other problem areas; Lana was more than happy to let Shawn handle it. She had much more pressing things on her mind. She had a mystery of a missing window to uncover.

CHAPTER EIGHT
The Marlow Ghosts

Lana raced down the stairs to the roll-top desk in the living room. After she'd finished clearing it of Mr. Marlow's papers, she'd set up her computer there. Pulling up a search engine, she typed in: *Percival Winston Marlow III.*

Her eyes scanned the long list of results. It wasn't a very common name, so each result seemed to be about the correct Mr. Marlow. She scrolled through the various articles, most of which were from their local paper. The paper had been around since the town was first founded. Over recent years, they'd digitized all of their old articles, even those from a hundred years earlier.

She read over the headlines:

PW Marlow's Toys & Collectibles Grand Opening.

Marlow Donates Toys to Children in Need.

Percival Marlow, Patron of the Arts.

Local Businessman Donates Rare Artwork to Museum.

Her breath caught in her chest when she read the next title listed. "*Are The Marlow Ghosts Real?*" she read the headline aloud. It was a much more recent article than the others; the date was only about ten years back. Heart racing, she clicked the link and began reading.

Percival Winston Marlow III was an eccentric, but well-liked, member of the community. A successful businessman and a supporter of the arts, he was respected and often praised. However, in 1910, shortly after the construction of his new home, he began speaking of ghosts roaming the halls of his country estate.

While the haunting of Percival Winston Marlow III was short-lived, it remained a local legend for years to come. Having no heirs, Mr. Marlow's estate and belongings were preserved by town officials in the years following his passing. Though there had been considerable interest in purchase, it was not sold for the first time until just six years ago; sixty years after Mr. Marlow's death. In the six years since the first sale, the estate has been bought and resold more than a dozen times, with no one staying in the house for longer than a single night.

When we reached out for comment from the previous owners, most were reluctant to recount their experiences. The one who was willing to speak with us said only, "There's something in the walls."

Lana reread the last line over and over again. "There's something in the walls," she whispered aloud.

"What?" Shawn's voice came from behind her. She heard the front door close and a truck start up in the drive. The electrician must have just left.

Lana stared blankly at Shawn for a moment, deciding what to say. She didn't want to tell him what she'd found, but he deserved to know. She pointed to the article still on her screen. As he read, she saw his eyes widen.

Shawn swallowed hard and took a deep breath.

Lana hesitated. "Are you moving out?" She braced herself for the answer.

Shawn made an exasperated groan, "... No..."

"Really?" Lana smiled.

Shawn looked a little defeated. "I can't leave you here alone. And I know you won't come with me."

"If you think about it," Lana began enthusiastically, "we've already lived here three times longer than anybody else. We've survived the banging on the walls, the hidden basement, the attic full of clowns..."

Shawn nodded. "True."

"The footsteps in the hallway," she added under her breath.

Shawn raised his eyebrows. "The *what* now?"

Lana shook her head. "Doesn't matter."

Shawn let out a heavy sigh. "I don't suppose the agent who showed you the place mentioned ghosts, or hauntings, or *why* all the previous owners fled after one day here?"

Lana pointed at the date on the screen. "The article is ten years old. It's possible they didn't even know about any of this. I mean, we grew up in this town and I've never heard anything about it. Have you?"

Shawn shook his head. "Pretty sure I'd remember something like that." He sighed and looked around the room.

"Marlow lived here for years," Lana reassured him. "If he found a way to deal with it, so can we."

Shawn didn't look convinced. "I guess I should call Nate and cancel my trip," he said, heading to the phone.

"What? Why?"

"I'm not leaving you here alone. What if the trip goes long? What if I'm gone for a month?"

"I'll be fine," she insisted. While she didn't like the fact that he'd be gone so long, she also didn't want to be the reason he gave up something he wanted to do. "I'll be at the shop during the day and I'll have Janey come stay with me on weekends."

"Would she do that?"

"Janey? Please, I mention ghosts and she might just move in. She *loves* this stuff."

Shawn seemed to relax. "Yeah, I know she really likes horror movies. I didn't know she was into actual ghosts, too."

"Sometimes I think the only reason she started a vintage shop with me was so she could find something that might be haunted."

Shawn laughed, "Yeah, alright. If Janey agrees, then I'll go."

CHAPTER NINE
Ghost Hunting

Lana paced up and down the hallway, floorboards creaking beneath her feet. She stared at the walls surrounding her. "There's something in the walls," she whispered as she ran her hand along the flowered paper print.

She knocked on the wall and pressed her ear to listen.

Nothing.

She knocked again. "Hello?"

Silence.

She continued pacing up and down the corridor, met by only the sound of her own steps walking through the hall. In all her walking she'd managed to figure out exactly which floorboards creaked and which didn't. She'd just about given up on rousing any ghosts.

"Is anyone there?" she called out one last time, knocking on the wall near the bathroom.

But this time... the wall knocked back.

Lana gasped, wide eyed and staring at the wall in front of her. She knocked again. It knocked back.

"Yeah?" she heard a voice call from the other side. Shawn stuck his head out of the bathroom door. "Are you just trying to scare me, or did you need something?"

CHAPTER ELEVEN
Rarities & Curiosities

Lana woke the next morning with the journal lying on the bed next to her. She thumbed through the ink stained parchment until she found where she'd left off. Sitting on her bed, she flipped through the pages of Mr. Marlow's journal. Page after page of musings on his life and business. Lana was looking over the entries when she caught sight of something that sounded familiar. Marlow wrote it about a week after he'd had the window removed.

A local curiosity shop thanked me for my donation to their store. If only they knew it was I that was grateful to them for taking that cursed window off my hands. As a gift, they sent along a toy for me to include in my own store; a most unfortunate looking jack-in-the-box. I've placed it in the attic with some other inventory. I don't think any of the children would care for such a creature.

Mr. Marlow had tucked the thank-you note from the curiosity shop neatly into the pages of the journal.

Our dearest Mr. Marlow,

We are delighted to have received your gift. It's exactly the kind of item that will fit right in at our little shop. We're certain that, in time, we'll find the perfect home for such a lovely piece. We pride ourselves on finding just the right place for unique items such as yours.

Lana looked a little embarrassed. "I might have been looking for a ghost," she admitted.

"Well, I'm taking a shower in here, so if you could raise the dead in a different part of the house, I'd appreciate it."

Lana retreated downstairs and to the kitchen. She marveled at how well Shawn was taking all of this. He'd made a lot of effort over the last few days to accept the house, even though it scared him. While he still teased her about the things she liked being *old garbage*, she could tell he didn't feel that way about everything. He loved Mortimer. And he even took a shine to the painting they'd found in the basement.

That painting. She could see it from across the kitchen. There, in its place on the living room wall. She stood slicing tomatoes for a dinner salad, still staring at the painting with the extra window. Now that she'd seen it, she couldn't unsee it. It called out for her attention. The window that shouldn't be.

She could smell the spaghetti sauce cooking on the stove. She pulled her eyes away from the painting, forcing herself to pay attention to what she was cooking. It was just a painting. Hidden in a basement. Behind a secret passageway. Locked by a wall sconce. She shook her head and focused on the boiling noodles on the stove.

Shawn came down to the kitchen holding Mortimer. "Whatcha burnin'?" he asked, placing the little jester next to him at the table.

She ran over to the oven and pulled the garlic bread out. Little puffs of smoke accompanied a strong smell as she brought the tray up to the counter. "I knew I forgot something!"

Shawn grabbed one of the smoldering breads and bit into the burned crust. "It's fine," he mumbled through bites.

Lana waved away smoke and eyed Mortimer. "You're not seriously going to have that thing at the dinner table?"

Shawn looked at the jester bouncing up and down in his box. "We're not welcome here, Mortimer," he joked.

"He's creepy," Lana explained.

"You bought a haunted house!" Shawn pointed a finger at her accusingly.

Lana laughed a little, "Alright, alright, he can stay."

Shawn smiled and took another bite of overcooked bread.

Lana walked over to a cupboard, opened the door, and promptly forgot what she'd been looking for. She stood, staring blankly at stacks of bowls and plates.

"Spaghetti strainer?" Shawn suggested, clearly noticing how distracted she was.

"Right." She reached in and grabbed a large colander. "Thanks."

"What's up with you?" he asked.

She paused for a moment, uneasy about revealing her worries concerning the painting. But that window was bothering her and it was going to keep bothering her. Shawn had already noticed. She might as well tell him. "There's something I should show you."

"I don't like the sound of that," he said, following her to the living room.

She showed him the extra window in the painting. She explained how she had compared it to the house and how it must have been in his room because his room was the closest to the front of the house. Then she stood in silence and waited for him to panic.

But he didn't panic. He laughed. "That's the least terrifying thing I've heard all day."

"It doesn't bother you?"

Shawn shook his head. "No. Lots of reasons to remove a window, Lan." He shrugged. "Maybe the sun was making his room too hot in the summer. Maybe the tree out front scraped against it when the wind blew. Maybe an animal outside was too loud, and he thought a more insulated wall would muffle it."

Lana was embarrassed. Those were all perfectly reasonable explanations, none of which had crossed her mind.

She laughed, "You're completely right. I guess, since so much weird stuff has happened, I just assumed this must be weird, too."

"Don't feel bad. I was doing the same thing with the light in my room. I was sure it was haunted."

"What was wrong with it?" Lana asked.

"Not sure. The electrician said the wiring to that sconce was *weird*. He said it looked like they added it after the others, and that's why it has its own switch. He tried to explain, but electricity is way over my head. Pretty sure he fixed it, though."

"That's good," Lana said.

"Yeah, honestly, I was just glad it didn't open any hidden doorways in my room when he started messing with it. Especially after he said it was added after the others."

"I mean, if there *were* a secret passage in your room, at least it wouldn't lead to a basement." She gave him a teasing grin. "You're on the second floor, so it would probably lead... to the attic."

"Very funny."

LANA WOKE TO WHISPERS all around her. She opened her eyes. The noise ceased the moment she sat up. "Hello?" she called out.

"Hello?" she heard a man's voice whisper.

She'd had enough of this. She wouldn't be harassed in her own home by anyone, not even a ghost. Lana climbed out from under her covers and raced toward her bedroom wall. She steadied her breath and listened. There it was again.

"Hello?" it whispered from within the walls.

She ran to the door and into the hallway. She made her way to Shawn's room. Maybe he'd heard it too. Lana carefully cracked open his door and peaked in. Shawn was asleep in his bed. Mortimer stood guard on the nightstand next to him. She closed the door.

"Who's there?" A voice shouted from down the hall. She looked, but there was nothing. She walked farther down the hallway and stood where the voice had been. This part of the hall was empty. No stairs, no doors, just dingy wallpaper and creaky floorboards. A loud banging rang out from the wall next to her. She put her ear to the wall, expecting to hear Shawn's snoring or the scraping of Mortimer's spring as he bobbed away next to Shawn's bed. But she heard none of that. Just a quivering, raspy breathing coming from inside the wall.

"Hello?" she whispered.

"Who's there?" The voice growled again. This time from within the walls.

Lana jumped back and gasped. There was no mistaking that for pipes.

She leaned back against the wall and listened. Those whispers were back, but they were clearer now. She could tell it was a man's voice, but it certainly wasn't Shawn. She knocked on the wall. The whispers gasped and hushed immediately.

"Percival?" Lana whispered. "Percival Marlow?" she was louder the second time.

Silence once more.

"Percival Marlow," she tried not to shout.

Silence still.

Lana returned to her room, confident that whatever was haunting their house was likely done for the night. It certainly didn't seem to want to talk to her anymore. Lana had no sooner climbed into bed when she heard a tapping on her bedroom door.

"I'm not afraid of you!" she shouted.

"I'm not afraid of you either," Shawn said back.

The door opened a little way, and through the crack popped Mortimer's head. The little bells on his hat jingled happily. "Are you afraid of me, Lana?" Shawn said in a silly voice.

Lana laughed and shook her head. "No, you're growing on me."

Shawn pushed the door open the rest of the way and smiled.

"What are you doing up?" she asked.

"Well, I was having this really great dream... that we lived somewhere else. Then I woke up to the sound of my sister shouting at a wall."

"Sorry about that."

Shawn shrugged. "Hey, I'm the last person who'll judge you for odd behavior," he said, pointing to Mortimer. "This place is stressful. You wanna scream at the walls, go for it."

"Thanks. I think I'm done for tonight," she assured him.

"Anything I should be worried about?" he asked.

"Nope. Honestly, I think the one in the hallway might be a little afraid of me."

"Nice," Shawn laughed. "Mind scaring them into a different house?"

"I'll do my best," she promised.

CHAPTER TEN
The Journal

Sunlight poured in through the living room window. The warm rays of soft light danced through the room, bouncing from surface to surface, and landing squarely on the painting of the house. Its wood frame glinted, showing off its fresh coat of polish. The colors were vibrant in the morning sun. Beautiful flowers and shrubberies that were no longer in the yard, immortalized in oil and canvas.

"I know how it sounds, but I heard it," Lana said.

"I hope it wasn't something lame, like pipes," came Janey's voice through the telephone receiver.

"No, that was the first thing I thought of. I spent days trying to convince Shawn and myself that's all it was. But there's no way this was pipes. It was all this talking and whispering in the walls."

"Ooh, maybe there's a body hidden in the walls!" Janey said, with far too much excitement in her voice.

"Janey!"

"Oh c'mon... you were thinking it."

Lana sat at the kitchen counter, pen in hand, mindlessly sketching the missing window on an old piece of paper. "Yeah," she laughed. "It crossed my mind... but Marlow built the house. I don't think he would have called so much attention to the haunting if he'd hidden a body in the walls."

"Maybe it was someone who died during construction. They were tragically crushed by a wooden beam. To hide the evidence, the foreman hid their body behind one of old man Marlow's walls, without him ever knowing. But now the soul of that man is doomed to forever roam your hallways, desperately searching for a way out of the home that became his tomb."

"Wow, Janey, that was elaborate."

Janey laughed, "I try."

"Doesn't explain the window, though. Or why someone would have it removed..."

"You think the window has something to do with the ghosts?" Janey asked.

"I don't know. It just bothers me," Lana explained. "Shawn had a lot of good reasons why someone would have removed it. They all made sense."

"But?"

"But there's something not right. I can just *feel* it. Every time I look at that window, something in me quivers."

"You have great instincts, Lana. Especially about antiques. Old is your wheelhouse. If your gut's telling you the window means something, then it probably does."

Lana stretched the coiled phone cord out behind her as she walked closer to the painting. "I'm a rich old man, and my house is haunted... why do I remove a window?" Lana said aloud, running her fingers across the painted window.

"Too bad you can't just ask him."

"Yeah..." Lana said, looking up at the ceiling. "Janey, I have to call you back."

Lana hung up the phone, eyes still fixed on the ceiling. A thought had struck her. A memory from the attic. "Maybe I *can* ask him," she said aloud.

LANA WALKED UP THE attic steps and headed straight for the old wardrobe. She'd completely forgotten about the journal she'd found with Mr. Marlow's name pressed into the leather cover. She hadn't read more than a few words before setting it down. But those few words were enough. *My home is finally complete.* Those were his words. The journal began with the completion of the house; there must be more inside.

She found the journal right where she had left it, tucked snuggly next to some large shoe boxes. She opened it and scanned the entries, flipping through pages of mundane thoughts. He talked about business, about charity work, occasionally about the Widow Constance that lived down the lane. Apparently, *her countenance held the sparkle of an unburdened spirit, despite her tribulations.*

Lana's eyes widened as she landed on an entry dated just days after the completion of the house.

Though I know I am alone in this house, I cannot deny I hear the sounds of another. I hear their footsteps in the halls. The sound of my own floors now mocks me.

She continued reading, skipping over the bits about new toy shipments and visits from old friends. There was another one, just two weeks after construction had finished.

The whispers... in the walls, from other rooms, at my door at night. I hear them all around me. As I lay in my bed, they call out. They will not let me sleep.

And another, a few days later.

It won't stop. The incessant noises, the creaking, the banging on the walls... Tonight, I steadied my nerves and resolved to face the beast at last. This demon. This blight on my home and life. I paced the halls of my home, demanding the creature reveal itself. But the coward hides within the walls.

Lana knew exactly how he felt.

And if these sufferings I've endured were not enough, there is that face. Each time I step out into my garden and gaze up at my windows, it's there. Always in the same window, staring directly back at me, the most horrifying look upon it. I can take no more. All the rest I could live with, but that face, that writhing, screaming face in my window... I can stand it no longer.

"A screaming face watching him from inside his own home..." Lana shivered. "No wonder he removed the window." She turned the page, eyes frantically searching for another entry about the window, or the face, anything at all. There it was, three days later.

I've had the contractor back. He was confused, but he did as I asked. All the rest is boarded up. Let the demon have it, but I'll not suffer even one more gaze at its twisted, screaming face. He's removed the wretched window. And the room it haunts is no more. Let this be the end of it.

"The room it haunts is no more," Lana whispered. Her mind reeled at the possibilities of that sentence. She raced down the attic stairs and into Shawn's room.

LANA STOOD IN SHAWN'S doorway, looking back and forth between his room and the hallway.

"What are you doing?" Shawn asked, staring at her from his desk.

"The hallway is longer than your room."

"So?"

"It extends way past where your wall ends," she explained.

Shawn gave her a confused look that told her he didn't understand the significance of what she was trying to tell him.

She handed him the journal. "Marlow was being haunted, too. He heard all the same things we have; the whispers, the footsteps; the banging on the walls. He wrote about all of it."

Shawn flipped through the pages of the journal. "Who's Widow Constance?"

"A neighbor. I think Marlow had a crush on her."

"Well, who could blame him? With *eyes of winter frost and cheeks that blushed of spring. Blooming of wisdom and of whimsy, betraying no signs of spite or sour nature.*" Shawn looked up from the journal. "She sounds like a keeper."

"Read the next entry," Lana said with a troubled expression.

Shawn turned the page and read. His eyebrows furrowed, and he looked up at her. "There's a writhing face staring back at him from inside the house?"

Lana nodded. "That's what he says. Every time he went outside he looked up and saw it."

"That's the window he had removed?"

"Seems so."

"Wait... *My* window? The thing that scared Marlow was in *this* room?" He stood quickly from his desk. He looked ready to run from the room.

"I don't think so," Lana reassured him. "Follow me."

Shawn still seemed uneasy, but he followed her down the hall. She stood staring at the extra piece of wall. It was large; easily the length of a room. She ran her hand across the wallpaper.

"I'm a rich old man, and my house is haunted... I don't just remove a window... I remove an entire room."

Shawn furrowed his brow. "What?"

"The window was never in your room, Shawn. Look," she pointed at the wall, "there's enough space left in the hall for another room."

"So you think there's a whole extra room behind that wall?"

Lana nodded. "He said *the room it haunts is no more.*"

"That's the same direction the weird noises have been coming from," he said, eyes fixed on the wall.

"Most of them," she agreed.

"Nah, I've seen this movie, Lan. The old man definitely killed someone and walled up their body."

"Then why write about it in his journal, or tell people about the ghosts?" Lana asked.

"The guilty conscience of a murderer. It was probably the widow's husband. Marlow wanted Constance for himself, so he killed her husband and hid the body here. And now he's trapped in our walls, desperate to take his revenge on whatever idiot opens that wall."

Lana hadn't thought about that. The *'guilt-ridden madman'* was a pretty popular theme in books from Mr. Marlow's time. Maybe a guilty man *would* do that.

"I'm telling you, Lana, all we'll find in there are bodies. And I really don't want to."

"Yeah, Janey said the same thing," she admitted.

"Janey knows her horror."

Lana nodded. "Yeah, I guess she d—"

The light nearest them began to buzz and flicker. It brightened to a blinding state, then suddenly turned off, leaving their section of the hallway dim. A clinking sound rattled from the other side of the wall. Like someone or something was chipping away at it, trying to make their way through.

"We should probably go," Lana said, but Shawn stood frozen. She grabbed his arm and pulled him toward his door. She pushed Shawn into his room and turned back to look at the empty hallway. The light was back on. The hall was quiet. She looked at Shawn, pale and terrified, in his doorway.

"See?" he said, pointing down the hallway. "Vengeful spirit!"

Lana looked back down the corridor. "I don't know if I'd call that *vengeful*, but it definitely wanted our attention."

"How did Marlow live with this?" Shawn asked, now clutching Mortimer.

She looked down at the journal still sitting on Shawn's desk. "I don't know, but I intend to find out." She retrieved the journal and headed back to her room with it. If Percival Marlow had managed to live there for twenty-four years, he must have figured out a way to silence his ghost problem. Lana just hoped he chose to write about it.

THE WINDOW IN THE PAINTING

As a thank you, we've included one of our odd little toys that you might like. We know he's not to everyone's taste, but we believe if anyone can help us find the perfect person for him, it's you.

Your friends and neighbors,

The Dreary Portent

Rarities & Curiosities

After this, the dates of Mr. Marlow's entries became far less frequent. There were weeks, sometimes years, between writings. He mentioned the Widow Constance several more times. Lana found herself especially disappointed when she came to the entry about the widow's wedding to a local barber. He maintained his composure, but the ink seemed somehow sadder in that passage.

Lana looked out her window. Her eyes were met with the dull, withered lawn of the side yard. A vast area of poorly maintained land stretched its way to the end of their property. In the distance, she could see a large manor house, about the same age as her own. She wondered if that could have been the widow's house. It seemed better cared for than hers. A green lawn, thriving trees, and a welcoming facade. It didn't seem at all haunted. Not from the outside, at least.

It had never occurred to Lana to go and meet the neighbors. To introduce herself to the people she'd be sharing a street with. She wondered if they all knew about the Marlow ghosts, or if they'd be as surprised as she and Shawn were.

She laughed. "Hi, I'm Lana. I bought the haunted house next door," she pretended into her mirror.

She'd never been very good at making friends. Even though owning a haunted house was interesting, it wasn't likely to help her win anyone over. Her introverted nature had never really bothered her. She had Shawn and Janey. That's all she needed. At the thought of Shawn, she sighed and glanced at the clock. Nine in the morning. Her stomach tied in knots. In twenty-four hours, Shawn would be heading to the airport. The thought of asking him not to go flickered into her mind for a moment, but she dismissed it as quickly as it had arrived.

LANA WALKED DOWNSTAIRS, still clutching the journal to her chest. Shawn was already in the kitchen sipping coffee.

"How'd you sleep?" he asked between bites of toast.

"Pretty good, actually. If anybody was whispering at me or walking around in the hallway, I was too tired to notice."

"Maybe that's Marlow's secret," Shawn suggested. "He didn't get rid of the ghosts; he was just too exhausted to notice them anymore."

"Well, that must have been it, because there's nothing in here so far." She plopped the journal down on the breakfast bar next to Shawn.

"Nothing?"

She shook her head. "He gets rid of the scary window, then he just stops talking about ghosts."

"That can't be all he did. We don't have the window and we've still got a bad case of haunted."

Lana shrugged and poured a cup of coffee. "I'll keep looking, but so far there's nothing helpful." She took a long sip from her mug. "Oh, I did find this, though. I think it's about Mortimer."

She opened the journal to the entry and the letter from the curiosity shop.

Shawn smiled. "That's kinda funny. These shop owners thought Marlow could find the perfect person for Mortimer, he hides him away in his attic, then a hundred years later, I find him."

"And you're his perfect person," Lana smiled. "Worked out nicely."

"Took some time, but yeah, it did." Shawn tucked the letter back into the journal. "Oh, I talked to Nate this morning."

"You're not still trying to cancel your trip, are you?"

Shawn shook his head. "No, but Nate said he'd pay for you to come with me."

"I thought we agreed I'd be fine?"

"Yeah, that was before the writhing faces and the people in the walls."

"Why would your boss agree to pay my way through Europe?"

"Because he's my friend, and he's your friend. And... because I told him my sister bought a haunted house and I don't want to leave her alone in it."

Lana rolled her eyes.

"He said he's been meaning to get you to look at some really old vintage film reels for him. So, if you'd be willing to do that while we're over there, he'll pay for you to go with me."

The temptation of vintage film reels was hard to resist. Even though she and Janey owned a clothing shop, virtually any kind of vintage or antique item was interesting to her. She also had to admit she'd been hesitant about being alone for so long. A house full of ghosts, plus Janey on the weekends, wasn't really the same as having Shawn there every day.

Lana started to agree; she *wanted* to agree. "I... I..." She sighed. "I can't."

"Why not?"

"It's not just the house. I have the shop. I can't leave Janey to run it on her own for that long. She's already been running it alone while we moved in here. I can't do that to her."

Shawn looked disappointed.

"I'll be fine," she assured him. She was a little disappointed, too. A European vacation on Nate's dime. Spending all her time in un-haunted hotel rooms, looking over vintage films. It sounded like a dream.

"Well, it was worth a shot," Shawn sighed. He stood up from his seat at the kitchen counter. "I guess I better start packing."

CHAPTER TWELVE
Shadows Pacing

No cleaning, no sorting, no boxing things up. It was Shawn's last day home and Lana was determined it was going to be fun. And while she may have thought sorting through old attic boxes was fun, she knew he didn't. Shawn finished packing his bag and stood in his room, holding Mortimer in one hand.

"Want me to leave him to protect you?"

"Janey will protect me. Mortimer protects you." Lana smiled at him from the doorway.

Shawn smiled back and stuffed Mortimer into his bag. "So, what's the plan today? It's not the attic again, is it? I know we still have a ton to sort through up there."

"Nope. No attic. No sorting at all." Lana held up a stack of movies. She'd found the box with all of Shawn's favorites and set up the TV in the living room.

"Are you sure? I don't want to leave you with all this work."

"Oh please. It's sorting through antiques. I love it."

Shawn grinned. "A little fun would be nice. This place has been pretty intense."

Shawn's favorite movies were all comedies. When it came to his work, he loved all genres; usually, the more artsy and angst filled, the better. But when it was for himself, comedy was just about the only genre he ever watched. A stack of Shawn's top six sat in front of them. One by one, the pile dwindled as they watched and laughed. Lana ran to the kitchen during the third film and made popcorn.

The day faded, the light dwindled, and their laughter filled the room. It was the first time since they'd moved in that Lana truly felt like this was their house. Not Percival Marlow's. Not a ghost's. Theirs.

Shawn yawned and reached for the last film. It was a supernatural comedy about a ghost who was miserable living with the new humans who moved into his house. "You know, maybe we skip this one."

Lana nodded in agreement. "A little too close to home. Plus, I don't want our ghost getting any new ideas on how to haunt us."

Shawn laughed. "I don't know; at least it'd be a lot funnier than just banging on the walls."

Shawn stretched and yawned again. "I have to get up early tomorrow. I better get to bed. Thanks for this, Lan."

Lana smiled. "Night."

"Night," Shawn said, and he disappeared up the stairs.

AS LANA CLIMBED THE stairs toward her room, she felt an odd surge run through her fingertips; like static electricity pulsing through the railing. A loud hum, then a sudden uncomfortable silence. She stopped just before the second floor landing. A shadow that was not her own hovered ominously at Shawn's door. It was faint and quivering. She likely wouldn't have even noticed it if it hadn't been for its haunting, voiceless whispers.

"What do you want?" She was careful not to wake Shawn, sleeping in his room.

The shade ignored her question and began to pace the hallway. It faded out of sight, but its footsteps remained. The lights flickered as the creaking footsteps passed them. Their inconsistent glow casting even more eerie, moving shadows in the hall. She couldn't tell how many there were, but she knew no earthly form was casting them.

The shade came back into view as it paced. It stood again at Shawn's door, but instead of whispering, it made a low mournful moan that echoed in Lana's ears. The way the shadow lingered near Shawn made Lana shiver. Whatever lurked in this house seemed far too interested in her brother. It was always his room, his wall, even his voice shouting her name. And now this shadow pacing at his door.

If something in the house really was a danger to Shawn, she felt some comfort in the fact that he'd be safely on his way to a film festival the next morning. Two weeks. That's how long she and Janey would have to figure out what was really going on. Shawn would be with Nate that whole time. He and Nate had been best friends for years. If she trusted anyone to look after Shawn, it was him.

Lana breathed a sigh of relief as the lights steadied themselves, eliminating the rogue shadow from Shawn's door. The hallway returned to normal. The house behaved as if nothing had ever happened.

CHAPTER THIRTEEN
Storm Clouds & Seances

Lana walked out into the murky, sunless morning. As she stood in the driveway, helping Shawn load the car, she couldn't help but notice that the house looked more grim than normal in the overcast light. The weather was bleak, and there was a sudden chill in the air that Lana hadn't expected. It had been warm for weeks.

Shawn put the last of his bags in the trunk of his car, just as another vehicle was pulling into the drive. It was a cute, sporty little car. Crimson colored. Lana had no idea what kind it was; cars weren't her thing.

Janey hopped out of the driver's seat. "Hello ghosts!" she shouted enthusiastically at the house.

Janey was smaller than average, adorable and petite, but her energy levels made her seem twice her size. She had long dark hair, twisted into two buns on the top of her head. She always wore her hair up to show off the heart tattoo on the back of her neck.

"This place is amazing!" Her dark eyes were wide, drinking in the spooky facade of the house. She reached into her car and hoisted an overstuffed backpack onto one shoulder.

"That's one word for it," Shawn said. "Probably not the word I'd use, though."

"Oh c'mon, Shawn. Look at this place. Didn't you expect it to be haunted?"

Shawn sighed and stared up at the house. "Actually, yeah. A little bit. Lana didn't though."

Janey cocked her head to the side. "Really?"

Lana shrugged. "Ghosts are more your thing. And apparently Shawn's."

Janey grinned at Shawn, "Cool! Had no idea you were into hauntings. We should go ghost hunting together!"

"No, no, no." Shawn backed away from her. "Not *into* them. I just believe in them."

Janey wrinkled her nose in obvious disappointment. "Bummer. Could have been fun, Shawny. Just you and me at the abandoned site of a serial murder, calling out to the tortured spirits of those who were viciously slaught—"

"Jeez Janey!" Lana interjected.

"Yeah, I think we have different ideas of fun." Shawn had a horrified look on his face.

"Yeah, probably," Janey laughed. "So, where's my room?"

LANA AND SHAWN SAID their goodbyes, and she watched as his car headed down the drive and out of sight. The sky was turning a dark shade of gray in the distance and heavy clouds were headed in their direction. She let out a sad quivering sigh and walked into the house. She led Janey through the living room and up the large wooden staircase.

"And this is your room," Lana said, slamming hard into the stubborn door of the spare room.

"Whoa." Janey marveled at the scene before her. Her eyes glinted with excitement as she admired the dusty, dilapidated room. She tossed her backpack onto the bed and strolled, grinning, around the room. Everything seemed to widen her smile; the peeling wallpaper; the small couch with the threadbare upholstery; even the torn and frayed curtains seemed to fill her with delight.

She peeked under a tattered sheet that was hiding a large, dingy dress form. "This would look amazing in the shop!"

"Really? It's pretty shabby, and the stand is broken."

Janey ignored her. "Whoa, look at this!" She ran over to a desk and pulled a worn, puffy footstool out from underneath. She moved it in front of the battered sofa and plopped down, propping her feet up on the footstool. "Nice." She smiled broadly at Lana.

"Well, if this impresses you, I can't wait to show you the rooms we actually use," Lana laughed.

Lana took Janey on a tour through the house, showing off her bedroom with the antique sewing machine, the lavish bathroom, and taking her up to the attic filled with antique toys.

Janey wound the crank on a jack-in-the-box and watched the jester pop out. She looked slightly disappointed. "They don't look that scary."

"They aren't," Lana explained. "The only scary one is Mortimer. He's different from the others. I think he came from a different shop."

"Cool. Where is he?"

"With Shawn. He offered to leave him, but he's so attached to that thing, I couldn't let him do that. Plus, honestly, one less weird thing in the house is probably fine."

"I'll have to see him when Shawn gets back. The way you described him on the phone, he sounds pretty great."

Lana held up one of the wooden clowns. "Are these not strange enough for you?"

"Aww, he's adorable!"

"My gift to you," Lana said, handing the clown to Janey.

"Are you sure? Antique toys are really expensive. You can probably get a lot for these."

Lana looked into the crate at the thirty-five clown faces staring up at her. "You know, I think I can spare that one."

THE GRAY CLOUDS OVER the horizon had rapidly made their way to the house. The sky outside was dark, brightened only when lightning flashed dangerously across it. The windows shook with each booming clap of thunder, as rain poured heavy over the roof.

Lana watched as Janey emptied her backpack out onto her bed. There were a handful of shirts, and socks, and other clothes; but mostly there were books. Half a dozen books on ghosts, hauntings, possession, and exorcism.

"I brought everything you asked for," Janey said, sorting through the pile. "Books, candles, sage..." She held up a small vial of greenish liquid. "I stole some water out of the fountain at the church by my house. I don't know if it's holy, but it's filled with algae. Maybe ghosts are afraid of algae."

Lana laughed. "Thanks."

"Mind telling me why I wasn't supposed to tell Shawn about this? He seems like he'd be pretty excited to get rid of the ghosts."

Lana hesitated. "I.. I think the spirits in this house might be after him."

"What? Why?"

"They're always by his door, or banging on his walls. Once I even heard one imitate him. It was using his voice to call my name. I'm just worried he's not safe here."

"Whoa." Janey looked troubled for the first time since she arrived. "Ghosts are cool and all, but if they're stalking Shawn, they're out of here." She grabbed a book on banishing spirits. "I was hoping we wouldn't need this one, but I say we evict these things."

"And how do we do that?"

Janey opened the book and thumbed through the worn pages. "First, we have to identify the entity. Then, if there's something it wants or is attached to, we can get rid of it that way. Otherwise..." She picked up a large bundle of sage and a lighter, "we cleanse its sorry soul!"

THE STORM CONTINUED to rage outside and Lana walked downstairs to find that Janey had filled the living room with lit candles. A large circle of them sat on the floor in front of the fireplace. A row stood lit on the mantle, illuminating Percival Marlow's portrait in an eerie, unappealing way.

"What's all this?" Lana gave Janey a suspicious look.

"I told you, we have to identify the entity. In order to do that, we have to have a seance. We'll call out to the spirits and find out why they're clinging to your house. And we can find out what's drawing them to Shawn."

Lana was all for banishing the ghosts in her house, but she was less certain about trying to commune with them. What few conversations she'd had with them so far had been fruitless. Mostly whispers and half sentences. But Lana had called Janey for help. If this was what Janey thought they should do, she had no choice but to go along.

"Fine. What do I do?"

"We have to sit in the circle," Janey explained. "Then we place our hands, palm to palm, and close our eyes."

Lana gave her an apprehensive look. "Then what happens?"

"Then I call out to the doomed spirits whose screaming, tortured souls have been trapped in your house for a hundred years."

Lana stared at her. "I'm not so sure I want to do that."

"Oh, c'mon. It'll be fun." Janey smiled and sat in the circle of candles. Lana hesitated briefly before joining her.

"We call to the spirit of Percival Marlow. Come to us!" Janey waited a moment and called again. "Percival Marlow! Show yourself to us!" Janey opened one eye and peered around the room. She pursed her lips. "Hmm..."

"Maybe he's shy," Lana laughed.

"I think we're calling out to the wrong spirit," Janey said. "Marlow was being haunted too, so let's see if we can get *that* ghost to come out." She closed her eyes and tried again. "Spirit of the house! Spirit trapped within these walls! We call out to you!"

A loud thumping noise erupted from outside. Tree branches scraped angrily against the sides of the house. They both looked around expectantly.

"It's just the wind," Lana whispered.

"Spirit of the house! Speak to us!"

More loud banging from outside. Lana couldn't tell where it was coming from. The wind was carrying the noises in all directions.

"Spirit trapped within these walls! Show yourself to us!" Janey commanded.

BAM! A loud booming thud rang out through the house as the front door swung open and crashed into the wall. Lana jumped and looked at the door. A shadowy figure loomed at the threshold. It lumbered forward and into the house.

Lana and Janey screamed and scrambled to get away from the hulking figure that inched its way toward them. The specter's face was cloaked with a dark hood and it dragged something large and formless across the floor, dropping it once it reached the living room. In the candle light Lana could see a smear of something liquid was oozing from the bundle the creature dragged.

The being spoke in a booming voice, "Lana..."

Lana shook and pressed herself back against the wall.

The spirit reached up and pulled its hood away, revealing its face.

CHAPTER FOURTEEN
You Should Sell Tickets

"Lana..." he repeated. "What are you two doing?"

Janey let out a small squeal, then started to laugh. Lana breathed a deep sigh of relief.

Shawn was drenched. His clothes and duffle bag were soaked in rain. He looked exhausted and confused. He pointed to the candles on the floor. "Did the power go out?"

Lana smiled. "Not exactly," she said, flicking on the lights.

"We were having a seance!" Janey said excitedly.

Shawn stared at them blankly for a moment. "A seance?"

Janey nodded, a smile beaming from ear to ear.

"Of course you were," he said, shaking his head. He looked at Lana. "I knew I shouldn't have left you."

"What *are* you doing back?" Lana picked up one of the candles and blew it out.

"Flight was canceled. Severe weather." He gestured outside.

Another figure appeared in the doorway, also cloaked and drenched. He tossed a suitcase on the floor and pulled off his hood. He was a little older than Shawn. Handsome. Dark hair slicked back with rain water.

"Hey, Nate," Lana smiled.

Nate smiled back. "Hey Lana. Hope you don't mind me crashing here. Bridge to my place is flooded out."

"The more the merrier." Lana blew out the last candle. As the flame vanished and the smoky tendrils drifted upward, a creaking sound came from above them.

The four of them stood staring at the ceiling as the creaking continued. The distinct sound of footsteps paced up and down the hall above them. Lana and Shawn looked at each other. Nate's brow furrowed as he continued to stare at the ceiling.

"Is there someone else here?" Nate asked, eyes still glued upward.

Shawn sighed. "You could say that."

Lana opened her arms hospitably. "Welcome to our haunted house. Enjoy your stay. Mind the ghosts."

Nate laughed and looked at Shawn. "Man, you weren't kidding."

THE HOUSE TREMBLED and shook in the heavy beating of the storm. Rain poured against the roof and windows in long, angry bursts. Morning arrived in a hazy gloom that made the whole house still feel like night. Lana crept into a barely lit kitchen. It seemed empty, but the smell of freshly brewed coffee let her know she wasn't the only one lurking through the house at six in the morning.

"You couldn't sleep either?" Nate's voice called from the darkest corner of the kitchen.

Lana shook her head. "First storm we've had since we moved in."

"Yeah, the trees, the wind, the creepy footsteps in the hallway..." Nate laughed. "You guys should sell tickets to this place."

"Not sure who'd buy them," Lana said, pouring her coffee.

"People like Janey." Nate smiled through the gray morning sun. "I'd have made breakfast, but I couldn't even find the light switch. Coffee was pretty easy, but I figured trying to cook in the dark would be a disaster."

Lana laughed and turned on the kitchen light. She and Nate grabbed the pans from the cupboard and began making breakfast for everyone. The smells of morning filled the house. Bacon, eggs, pancakes, Nate even made waffles. The counters were covered in plates of food.

It wasn't long before everyone else made their way down to breakfast. Janey came hopping down the stairs, seemingly well rested and full of her normal energy. "Don't you just love this weather?" She smiled. "Ooh! Pancakes!"

Shawn stumbled his way down the stairs, eyes still half closed, pajamas still on. "Why are you people up so early?"

"Why are you?" Lana asked.

He pointed to the plates of food. Shawn sat Mortimer on the breakfast bar while he grabbed a plate and stacked it with a little bit of everything.

Janey's eyes widened. "Is that Mortimer? He's amazing!"

Shawn smiled. "You hear that, Mortimer, you're famous."

Mortimer bobbed politely as Janey jingled the bells on his hat and grinned at him.

Nate leaned in close to Lana. "It's not my imagination, right? That little puppet thing is terrifying?"

"Not your imagination. Mortimer is the thing nightmares are made of," Lana whispered back.

"I can hear you," Shawn said. "And so can Mortimer," he warned.

Lana laughed. Nate seemed a little unnerved. "He grows on you after a while," she promised. "That or he's slowly taking over my mind with his horrific, unblinking stare..."

"You've been spending too much time with Janey," Nate teased. But his grin quickly faded as Shawn turned the crank on Mortimer's box and the eerie backward music rang out across the kitchen.

NATE PACED BACK AND forth through the kitchen, wrapping himself in the telephone cord as he tried to cancel his reservations. He had booked everything in advance; cars, flights, hotel rooms. But the storm wasn't letting up and there was no way they'd make it to the film festival in time. The trip was off.

Lana watched from the couch as Nate untangled himself from the phone cord and made his way into the living room. "Get everything sorted?" she asked.

He sighed and nodded. "Pretty sure. Everything except the hotel. I had to use an automated system to cancel, and I have no idea if it went through or not." He looked out at the rain, huge drops slamming hard against the window glass. "I called my neighbor too. She said the bridge is still flooded," he looked at Lana and smiled, "so you're stuck with me for a while."

Lana smiled back. She'd known Nate for years; she loved having him around. And she couldn't have been happier to have Shawn home. But still, she found herself worrying. She and Janey had never gotten a chance to investigate the house. They hadn't learned anything about the spirits or why they might be drawn to

Shawn. If they even were. Maybe she was overreacting. She needed to talk to Janey.

Lana went upstairs to find Janey's door wide open, letting a soft spicy scent drift through the hall. Janey was sitting on her bed, looking through one of the books she'd brought. A bowl of sage was lightly smoking on the dresser.

"What do you think is scarier," she asked without looking up from her book, "a poltergeist or a doppelganger?"

"What's the difference?" Lana asked.

"A poltergeist throws things around, a doppelganger impersonates someone alive."

Lana flashed back to hearing Shawn's voice calling to her from the hallway while the real Shawn slept downstairs. "Doppelganger, definitely."

"Have you noticed any apparitions?"

"You're going to have to explain that one, too," Lana admitted. "I'm not really up to date on my paranormal terminology."

Janey smiled. "The physical form of the ghost. Like, have you actually *seen* one?"

"Just a shadow, but never an actual form of a person."

"Hmmm..." Janey seemed disappointed.

"Marlow did though."

Janey perked up. "Really?"

"Yeah. That's why he removed the window. Every time he went outside, he saw a face in the window, screaming from inside the house. So he had the window removed, and the room sealed off."

"Whoa." Janey's eyes widened. "So there's a hidden room with a ghost in it somewhere in this house?" She looked around the room. "I wonder where it is?"

"Oh, we know where it is. You wanna see?"

Janey nodded and bounded up off the bed, grinning.

Lana led Janey down the hall to where she believed the room had been. "Behind this wall."

Janey stared at the wall, a look of awe on her face. "That is so cool."

"I wanted to open it up, but Shawn wouldn't let me."

"He's right," Janey agreed.

Her words took Lana by surprise. She was sure that Janey, of all people, would be excited about the idea of opening a secret room potentially filled with ghosts. "You afraid it's full of bodies, too?" she asked.

"I'm afraid it's full of bugs and spiders." Janey shivered a little at the mention.

Lana could hear Shawn and Nate talking and laughing downstairs. "Should we try the seance again tonight?"

"Nah," Janey began walking back to her room, and Lana followed. "I've been reading up on the types of ghosts that haunt old houses like this. Since Marlow built the house, I don't think it's someone who died here. I think it's someone who's attached to the house, or maybe attached to something *in* the house. But it's impossible to know which."

"So what do we do?"

Janey pointed to the bowl of sage on the dresser. "The sage clears the energy from the house. But since we don't know what the spirits are attached to, we just have to cleanse as much as we can and hope that does the trick."

Lana looked over at the soft haze rising from the bowl on the dresser. All of her hopes now hinged on those swirling, scented curls of smoke.

CHAPTER FIFTEEN
The Man On The Phone

Lana walked through the hallway and down the stairs. The air was thick, and a peculiar fog hung eerily all around her. The staircase felt longer than usual; or maybe she was slower, but it seemed like ages walking further and further down into the heart of the house. She could hear something in the distance. A bell? A chime? No... a phone. The phone in the kitchen was ringing.

She finally made her way through the dense, milky air of the living room and into the kitchen. The phone pierced the air, louder than ever. It was screaming a shrill, violent ring. The receiver weighed heavy in her hand as she picked it up. Everything seemed suddenly harder and more exhausting. She held the phone to her ear.

"Hello?" she said, but her voice was small.

Silence.

"Hello?" she croaked again. She could barely speak.

Horrible whispers filled the other end of the line. Voices on top of voices all swirling together; raspy tones that seemed both hushed and shouting at the same time.

"What do you want?" she tried to scream.

The voices kept whispering in a mangled mess of sounds; she listened harder, desperate to make sense of anything they were saying. Then one hushed and garbled voice rose slightly above the rest. The only words she could understand. *"Where are you?"* the voice cried out.

Lana woke with a start and sat up in bed. It was morning. A tiny trickle of gray-blue light was creeping in through her curtains as the storm blocked any chance of sunshine. She stood from her bed, exhausted. She'd tossed and turned all night, her head full of nightmares. It wasn't like her to be so worried and anxious.

She looked around her room; a room she'd loved when they first moved in. But it felt different now; dark and gloomy. It wasn't just the storm making it look that way. There was a feeling of dread hanging in the air. She still loved the house, but she feared it didn't feel the same about her and Shawn.

THE STORM OUTSIDE BEAT on every wall and window. As Lana came down the stairs, she could hear the wind whipping through the gnarled trees and a steady pour of rain. The others were already up and standing around the kitchen, laughing and talking. Through the smell of brewing coffee, Lana caught an odd scent she couldn't quite identify.

"Morning," Lana said, trying to sound as though she'd slept.

"Morning," Shawn said through bites of breakfast. Nate flashed a smile.

"I made breakfast," Janey announced, handing her a box of cereal.

"This is your idea of making breakfast?" Lana smirked.

Shawn laughed. "No, *that* was her idea of making breakfast." He pointed to a still smoldering pot on the stove.

"We stopped her before she caused any real damage." Nate gave Lana a grin and a wink. "But it was too late to save the oatmeal."

"May it rest in peace," Shawn laughed.

Janey rolled her eyes. "It wasn't that bad. We still could have had it, but they refused to even taste it."

Shawn held up the pot, showing the blackened mess inside. "You first," he said looking at Janey.

Janey started to say something, but was interrupted by the phone. Its loud vibrating tone shot through Lana like ice water. Her mind flashed back, remembering that horrible nightmare. The hushed voices licking at her ears.

Lana stared at the ringing phone, frozen.

"You gonna get that?" Shawn asked.

"Yeah," she said. "Of course..." She reached over and grabbed the receiver, placing it to her ear.

"Lana?" The voice on the other end was broken and weak. "Lana..." There was a sad, strained tone behind it, but there was no mistaking it was Shawn's voice.

She looked up at Shawn standing in front of her, while his voice cried out her name on the other end of the phone line. She stared, unblinking. Her breathing shallowed. Everyone seemed to notice.

Shawn narrowed his eyes. "What's going on?"

She couldn't answer. She couldn't speak. All she could do was listen to the cracked and weary voice calling her name over and over.

Nate took the phone from her and listened for a moment, his eyebrows furrowed. He swallowed hard and put the receiver back on the hook.

"Who was it?" Shawn asked.

Nate looked pale. "It was you."

Lana felt oddly relieved that Nate had heard it, too. She and Shawn had experienced so much that would seem unbelievable to anyone else. But she could tell by the look on Nate's face that he believed them.

Shawn didn't say anything at first. He just stared. Silent. Scared. "Why do they keep using my voice?"

"What do you mean, *keep* using it? Has this happened before?" Nate asked.

Lana nodded. "A couple of nights after we moved in. I heard him calling me from his room. He sounded really scared, so I ran to check on him, but... he wasn't in his room. He was downstairs... asleep."

"I don't wanna scare you, man, but that seems like a really bad omen." Nate looked nervously at the rain beating against the window. "When this storm passes, maybe you should come stay with me."

Shawn didn't have a chance to respond.

RING! RING! RING! RING!

All four of them stared at the phone.

Lana was afraid to move. "Maybe we shouldn't—"

"Hello?" Janey said, grabbing the phone.

Janey sat, silent, holding the phone to her ear. She didn't respond; she simply listened and then carefully hung up the phone.

She looked Nate square in the eye. "It was for you," she said ominously. "The ghosts said to tell you... your hotel cancellation has been confirmed."

"Cute." Nate looked annoyed.

Janey burst out laughing. "Hey, you got to talk to a ghost, and all I got was a lousy automated message."

THE WINDOW IN THE PAINTING

SHAWN STARED OUT THE living room window, watching the rain pour down against the roof of his car. He'd been quiet all afternoon. Lana watched him for a moment, unsure if she should bother him.

"Hey," she finally said from behind him. "You alright?"

He nodded, but didn't look away from the window. "This place is cursed." There was a seriousness that was strange to his voice.

"Well, it'll be someone else's problem soon," she promised.

He turned around to look at her, his expression seemed surprised. "What do you mean?"

"I'm selling it."

"Really?" he asked. He tried to mask it, but she could see the relief on his face.

"Really. I mean, I don't care how good of a deal I got on the place, I can't keep a house that doesn't let me sleep and keeps trying to doppelganger my brother."

Shawn forced a laugh. "At least now we know why it was so cheap."

"Yeah, I thought it was great that we stayed so much longer than the previous buyers... turns out they had the right idea."

"You break the news to Janey yet?" Shawn asked. "She's gonna be heartbroken."

Lana nodded and laughed. "She asked how much I want for the place."

Shawn raised his eyebrows. "Sell it to her," he said, finally stepping away from the window. He seemed more relaxed now.

Lana and Shawn joined the others in the kitchen. Janey was talking animatedly about something, and Nate was listening intently.

"Wait, why do you need me for this?" he asked.

"Because I can't afford it by myself. But if we go in on it together, then I can."

"But I don't want to own half a haunted house," Nate argued.

Janey groaned. "It's an *investment opportunity*, Nate."

"An investment in what?"

"In my dream of owning a haunted house!" Janey explained.

"I'm gonna pass, thanks."

Shawn looked at Lana. "*Sell it to her*," he repeated.

Lana looked at Janey's pleading face and sighed in quiet defeat. She looked around the house. "I mean, this place *is* full of antiques. If I sold a few things, I could lower the price to something Janey could afford. The stuff in the attic alone would probably be enough."

Janey's eyes lit up. "Yes! Yes! Sell everything in the attic! I told you those toys are worth a fortune."

Shawn looked at Mortimer sitting on the breakfast bar and slowly scooted him away from Lana.

Lana smiled. "Relax, I'm not selling Mortimer. He's found his forever home with you."

CHAPTER SIXTEEN
Four Bedroom, One Bath

After days of rain dwindled down to a slow drizzle and the wind finally settled, Lana was pleased to see the sun had decided to make an appearance. She looked out the living room window to see that some of the water had cleared away from the drive.

Lana looked up toward the ceiling as a raucous banging came pounding from above her. Another loud thud followed by angry, muffled cursing.

"Careful! This thing's like a hundred years old. Lana will kill us if we ruin it!" Shawn shouted.

Lana looked up to see Shawn and Nate thumping their way down the stairs, carrying Shawn's steamer trunk down into the living room. They came to a stop in the foyer, setting the trunk down with the rest of Shawn's belongings.

"That everything?" Lana asked.

Shawn nodded sadly.

"Living with Nate for a while will be fun," Lana reassured him. "He's a great roommate."

"And I have exactly zero ghosts in my house," Nate promised with a grin.

Shawn smiled. "I do really like that in a roommate." He looked back at Lana. "I just don't like leaving you here."

"I know, but it's only temporary. Once I get the antiques sold, you and I can move someplace new and completely unhaunted."

Shawn forced a laugh, but he still looked worried.

"Plus, I won't be alone," she reminded him. "Janey's moving in, so she'll be here most of the time."

"I still can't believe she's buying this place," Nate said, tossing his own suitcase onto the pile of Shawn's luggage. He turned and looked back around the house. "I don't know who I'm more afraid for, Janey or the ghosts."

"Definitely the ghosts," Lana smiled. "They've met their match with her."

Nate smiled at Lana. "You know, there's room for you at my place. You don't have to stay here."

"That's tempting," she admitted. "But it's just easier to sort through everything if I'm here."

His smile faded a little as he looked at her. "Offer's always open." There was a sweet, genuine tone to his voice. He hoisted two of Shawn's bags over his shoulders and headed outside.

Lana wanted to say yes. Being there with Shawn and Nate sounded miles better than being in a house full of whispering shadows and light-flickering spirits. She looked around the house and sighed at the sheer volume of items she had left to go through. As much as she wanted to take Nate up on his offer, everything would go faster if she stayed where she was. Life outside the house would have to wait.

THE WINDOW IN THE PAINTING

LANA WATCHED FROM THE attic window as Shawn and Nate drove away. After struggling with the steamer trunk for twenty minutes, they finally realized it wouldn't fit in Shawn's car and put it in Nate's instead. Lana couldn't help but feel a little sad as she watched their cars disappear out of the driveway and down the road. They were only a few minutes away, but it felt so much farther.

"Why didn't you go with them?" Janey appeared next to her at the attic window.

"What?"

"I heard them talking about it at the car," Janey said. "Nate offered to let you stay at his place. Why didn't you?"

"Don't you want me here?" Lana asked.

"Of course! But it's not about where *I* want you to be, it's about where *you* want you to be. And right now, that look on your face says you'd rather be in the car on your way to Nate's."

Lana gestured to the attic around her. "Once all this is done, then I can worry about where I'll go next."

"Well, then we better get started, so you can stop all your worrying, and just decide where you want to be." Janey smiled and began sorting through the box nearest her.

"You don't have to do that," Lana said. "It's my responsibility to sell all this. It's way too much work to ask you to help."

"You're doing this so that I can afford to buy the house. The least I can do is help you sort through it all," Janey reasoned.

Lana was grateful for the help. As much as she loved sorting through old antiques, she was anxious to be done. Janey was right; if Marlow's house wasn't meant to be her home, she wanted to find a place that was. The sooner everything in the attic was sold, the sooner that could happen.

Sorting was much quicker with two people. Before she knew it, she and Janey had hauled half the attic contents downstairs and neatly arranged them in the foyer. She placed a box on the stack and headed back up to the attic where Janey was enthusiastically sorting through some paintings piled behind a crate of toys.

"Hey, look at this!" Janey called out. She was holding up a large painting of a regal-looking dog. "Look at the signature."

Lana immediately recognized the scrolling, elegant signature in the corner. "Percival Marlow," she said under her breath, tracing the delicate lines of his signature with her finger. "This must be Duke. Marlow talked about him a lot in his journal. He's beautiful."

"Here's another one of his!" Janey held up a serene-looking landscape.

Lana looked down at the stack of paintings and realized that several of them bore Marlow's signature. The walls of the house were full of paintings, but Lana had only ever seen one that was made by Marlow. His work was beautiful; he'd clearly been more than just an admirer of the arts.

As Lana made her last trip downstairs for the night, carrying boxes of odds and ends to stack with the others in the foyer, she passed by the painting of the house, hung in its place in the living room. She couldn't help but wonder why Marlow would store all of his other paintings in the attic together, but hide that one away in a secret basement, left to the whim of the elements. Perhaps he was afraid that if the ghost couldn't show itself in the actual window, it might make use of a painted version instead.

She sat the boxes down, eyes still fixed on the canvas, poring over all the little details. She ran her fingers over the small painted window, trying to imagine what a writhing, screaming face might look like. Lana stared at the paint, searching every brush stroke, every crack, every slight run of paint, to see if there was any hint of what he'd seen reflected in his work.

But there was nothing. Every detail remained exactly in place. No sign or trace of any ghosts, in the window or otherwise. Lana walked away, leaving the painting where it hung. She didn't have the heart to sell it; it was one of the few things in the house Shawn actually liked.

CHAPTER SEVENTEEN
The Widow Constance

The next few days were an exhausting blur. The foyer was piled with boxes and paintings all ready to be picked up. She and Janey had found an auction house in town that was more than happy to help them find new homes for Mr. Marlow's belongings.

Lana carried the large painting of the dog down from the attic and sat it in the living room next to the boxes of things ready to go to auction. "Sorry puppy, you're adorable, but I doubt I'll have a place for you when we move."

Out of the corner of her eye she could see Janey in the kitchen, pacing. She was on the phone, talking animatedly to someone. She seemed excited.

Janey hung up the phone and ran into the living room. "I just got a call from the event planners. We're outfitting a costume party they're putting together and the customers want to pick up everything tonight. I've got to run in and open up for them."

"A whole party-worth of people sounds like a lot of work. Let me come help."

"It's no big deal. They've been in a bunch of times this week picking things out and having me set things aside for them." Janey said. "They're basically just paying and taking their stuff."

"Still, I feel like I should help," Lana argued.

"No way. I gave you two weeks off; you're going to take every single day of it. You already gave up a free trip to Europe for me. Which was crazy, by the way. You absolutely should have ditched me for Europe."

Lana laughed. "That trip ended up canceled anyway, so it wouldn't have mattered if I'd said yes."

"I know," Janey shrugged, "but now you're moving again and trying to get all these antiques sold... The least I can do is make sure you have a few more days where you don't have to worry about work."

"You're a good friend."

"I insist you remember that when you price the house," Janey laughed as she headed out the front door.

Lana went upstairs and brought down several unsorted boxes from the attic. Normally she would work up there, but the air had gotten chilly. She started a fire and began the rest of the sorting in the living room, where it was warm. She hated to admit it, but she also found herself not wanting to be alone in the attic. Lana had teased Shawn about his fears, but now that she knew the house had actual ghosts, suddenly attic demons didn't seem so farfetched.

LANA CONTINUED SORTING through the haul from the attic; boxes of antique baubles. As she was deciding what to sell and what to keep, she spotted Mr. Marlow's journal on the desk. Lana picked up the journal and ran her fingers over the pressed name in the leather. PW Marlow III.

In a weird way, she was going to miss him. A local museum would probably love to have the journal, but Lana found herself a little attached to it. She opened the cover and thumbed through the pages until she reached where she'd left off.

"It'd be a shame not to finish it."

Lana curled up in a chair by the fireplace, journal in hand, poring over the entries. She hadn't even realized how long it had been until the phone rang, forcing her eyes away from the inky pages. She walked to the kitchen to answer the phone, turning on the light as she passed the switch.

"Hey. Sorry this is taking so long," Janey's voice said from the other end of the phone.

"It's fine."

"It's gonna be a little longer. They just spotted those suits you sent over and they love them. They're picking out which ones they want. One guy is even buying the cuff links."

"Wow! Yeah, it's no problem. Everything's good here. I'm just reading a book."

"You sure?" There was a little worry behind Janey's voice.

"Completely," Lana assured her.

Lana hung up the phone and returned to her seat by the fire. She picked up the journal and turned to the next entry. She immediately wished she hadn't.

The Widow Constance is dead.

Lana gasped.

Her joyous face shall no more greet me with a kind hello as I take my evening stroll. The flowers in her garden may forever bloom, but she has taken with her a bit of their luster. Their color not so bright, nor their smell so sweet, as when she stood by their side.

Lana's eyes teared up a little as she read and she let out a small sniffle.

THE WINDOW IN THE PAINTING

And though she was not mine to love, my heart feels it all the same. I regret now more than ever the loss of her portrait, walled within a room I no longer touch nor dare to think of. I removed nothing from that cursed room before I exiled it from my sight. Everything within it could be replaced, everything except her face. What I would not give to look upon her fair visage again, even if only a painted image. But I cannot dare to open that room. Not even to see my sweet Constance one last time. My heart weeps.

CHAPTER EIGHTEEN
It Was Hidden For A Reason

Lana stared at the wall in the hallway. Behind it lived a portrait of Widow Constance. A portrait so precious to Percival Marlow that he regretted its loss for years to come. Even in her death, he couldn't bring himself to open the wall and see her face. Marlow didn't want the haunting to start again, but for her and Shawn, the haunting had never stopped. What difference could unsealing the room possibly make if the ghosts were already loose in the house?

Shawn was afraid they'd find a body in the wall, but Lana didn't believe that Percival Marlow had killed anyone. Janey's story about the construction worker had been imaginative, but she didn't really believe that either.

She ran her hand across the wallpaper until she reached a seam where two pieces came together. Lana dug her nails into the seam, trying to get a finger-hold. A small section of the paper gave in to her and lifted from the wall. Peeling back the paper revealed a section of the wall that was more than simply boards and plaster, it was brick.

There was a section of the brickwork that was worn and crumbled. It had a large crack that seemed as though it might give with enough pressure. The entire thing looked as though Marlow had put it together hastily. In fairness, he probably had.

Lana ran to the tool cupboard in the laundry room and searched for something that could help her open the wall. Even if she couldn't get in, if she could at least see what was on the other side, she'd know if it was worth it to take the wall down completely. She spotted an old hammer with a wooden handle.

"You'll do."

Lana tapped on the wall with the hammer, careful not to bring the entire thing down. She just needed a hole large enough to see inside. She hit the cracked section again; several chunks of brick crumbled and fell into the space behind the wall. She shined her flashlight inside, but wasn't able to see anything yet. She swung the hammer again. More pieces crumbled away. She could see there was a large space behind the wall, but she still couldn't find an angle that allowed her to see inside the room.

Lana eyed the hole she'd made. It was larger than she'd intended it to be. Surely she was small enough to squeeze through. She grabbed her flashlight and Marlow's journal and crawled her way through the dusty, crumbling wall. She'd only just gotten her head and shoulders through when she felt the wall give and start to collapse around her.

Lana heard the wooden boards breaking in her ears. She fell headfirst through the brick and plaster. Mr. Marlow's journal leapt from her grasp, tumbling away from her as she toppled through the wall. She heard the bricks collapse behind her, sealing off the entrance she'd made. She pulled herself to her feet and looked back at the wall. "You've got to be kidding me."

Lana tried not to panic. It was fine. Janey would be home soon. She'd call Shawn and Nate for help, and the three of them would have her out of there in no time. She took a deep breath and calmed herself. She just had to wait for Janey. Until then, she might as well have a look around.

She lifted up some nearby bricks and debris from the floor, searching for the journal she'd dropped when she fell. But it wasn't there. She knew she had it as she came through the wall. "Where are you?" she shined her flashlight on the floor, though she didn't really need it. The room was fairly bright.

It only took her a moment to spot what she'd come for. There, hung on the wall, was a portrait of a stunning and stately woman.

"Look at you..." Lana said, walking closer to the painting.

She was beautiful. Her hair was dark and adorned with golden combs. She was far younger than the name *Widow Constance* had suggested. Lana examined the painting for damage; it seemed to be in perfect condition. Janey would be pleased to know that there were no bugs in sight. There didn't seem to be any bugs or spider webs anywhere in the room.

She turned off the flashlight and sat it on a small nightstand. The nightstand was exactly like the one by Shawn's bed. As a matter of fact, the bed was exactly like Shawn's as well. Everything in the room was identical to Shawn's room. Same dresser, same desk, same mirror that had scared her the night they first moved in.

She walked over to the sconce on the wall. "Do you burn out every night, too?" She ran her finger across the dusty bulb. She felt a slight shock of electricity. "Ow!" As she pulled her hand away, she heard a loud pop come from Shawn's room. His light had burned out again.

As she moved closer, she heard something else coming from Shawn's room. She pressed her ear to the wall. It was a voice.

"Not again!" Shawn's voice shouted from his bedroom.

Shawn was home. He must have decided to come back. She knew he'd be upset that she went in there, but it didn't matter. She was so excited that he was home. Lana listened again, hoping he hadn't left his room yet.

"I just replaced that bulb and it's burned out again. What is going on with it?" she heard him say in a muffled voice.

Lana banged on the wall. "Shawn! Shawn! I'm stuck in here! Can you hear me?"

"What was that?" Shawn asked.

"Probably just pipes," a woman's voice answered from in the room with him.

"It's not pipes, it's me!" Lana shouted. She banged hard on the wall again.

"That was not pipes." Shawn sounded scared. "I'm sleeping downstairs tonight."

Lana pulled her ear away from the wall. The conversation on the other side was starting to sound eerily familiar. "It might be a spooky ghost..." Lana whispered under her breath, then listened again.

"Yeah, best to be safe. It might be a spoooooooky ghost," the woman laughed.

"Not funny, Lan!" Shawn's voice shouted from the hallway.

Lana pulled her ear away from the wall and shook her head in disbelief. A chill ran over her. "No way. There's no way that was us."

She looked at the wall, remembering that night. Remembering walking up to the wall. Lana ran her fingers across the crumbling paint. "It was never pipes..." she whispered.

Lana couldn't believe what she was hearing. She sat on the bed, somewhere between shock and panic. Then she looked up and saw why this abandoned room was so bright. Light shone in from the summer sun through a large window. A window that shouldn't be there. A window that had been removed from the house a hundred years earlier.

"No..."

She raced to the window and looked outside. It was a clear sunny day with a perfect view of a magnificent front garden. Flowers in bloom, trees alive and flourishing. A familiar-looking dog ran playfully across a lush green lawn. She'd seen him before, in a painting in the attic. In the drive sat an antique car. But it didn't look old at all. It was perfect and new. And standing next to it was Percival Marlow.

She screamed and begged for his attention, fists pounding on the glass as she shouted and cried out. He looked up and caught her eye, his face contorted in fear at the sight of her. At first, she didn't understand why he seemed so afraid. He shook his head and backed away in terror. And then Lana realized why...

Percival Marlow wasn't looking up at a girl he'd never seen before, trapped in a room of his house. He was staring up at the writhing, screaming face of the woman that haunted his home. The woman who paced his hallways, who knocked on his walls, who called out his name in the dead of night.

She stood at the window, face twisted in fear and desperation. There was nothing more that she could do...

CHAPTER NINETEEN

Shawn

Shawn walked in the door, uncertain of what he was going to find. He saw Janey sitting on the moth-eaten sofa, crying. He saw Nate consoling her.

"We've checked the whole house, man. I don't know where she could have gone," Nate said, walking over to him. "Janey called me when she couldn't get a hold of you. I thought maybe she just went into town or something. She'd been trying to sell all this stuff." Nate pointed to the boxes by the front door.

"But I called the auction house and they haven't talked to her either," Janey sobbed.

Shawn didn't say anything at first. His mind couldn't process what was happening. He'd been screening movies all day when Janey tried to call him. As soon as he heard her message, he drove straight over, but he half expected Lana to be there when he got to the house. Like it had all been a misunderstanding. He looked around the living room.

Shawn furrowed his brow. "You checked the whole house?" he asked.

"Everywhere," Janey promised.

His eyes narrowed on the sconce across the room. "Are you sure?"

"Yeah, man, every room. Plus the attic." Nate looked confused at the question.

Shawn walked across the room and pulled on the bulb-less sconce. The metal mechanisms in the wall whirred and scraped against one another. He'd sworn he'd never open that door again, but if Lana had gone back down there, it was worth checking.

Janey and Nate stared in disbelief as the wall opened in front of them, revealing the rickety, broken staircase below. The smell of damp and mildew wafted up from the darkness. Shawn shined a flashlight into the hidden room, hoping to see a sheepish Lana staring up at him, embarrassed to have gotten herself locked in the basement. But she wasn't there. Shawn shined the light on every crate and cobblestone, but nothing looked changed or disturbed.

"What is this?" Janey asked.

"Secret basement," Shawn said plainly. He walked over and pushed the sconce back into place, closing the hidden door. He gestured to the portrait of Percival Marlow. "He had it built into the house."

"This place is so weird." Nate shook his head and leaned against the arm of the sofa.

"Are there more of those?" Janey asked.

"Not that we found." The light in the living room was slowly dwindling away. Shawn looked out the window at the approaching night. "I have to stay here. I can't leave until I find her." His voice cracked as he spoke.

"I know." Nate pointed to a duffle bag and a suitcase sitting by the stairs. "We're all staying."

"We have to find her." Shawn's voice was quivery and quiet.

"Listen, it's late and you're exhausted. Try to get some sleep. We're here now." Nate put a reassuring hand on Shawn's shoulder. "We'll find her, Shawn."

He nodded and headed up the stairs toward his room.

Shawn walked into his bedroom and dropped his bag on the floor. He sat Mortimer down next to his bed. His hat bells jingled with a somber tone as he bobbed sadly on the nightstand.

Shawn sighed. The house had an odd, empty feeling to it. Everything was exactly the same as when he'd left, but something was definitely different. He heard the scraping sound of the door frame to her room as Janey turned in for the night.

Shawn sat on his bed and closed his eyes. He listened to the silence of the house. It was deafening. That was the difference. *That's* what had changed. An eerie hush lingered in the air. The house was never silent, always creaking and banging; gurgling groaning noises traveling through the walls and filling every room. But they were gone, leaving only this empty, heavy quiet in their place.

He looked at his wall. The wall that had once frightened him into sleeping on a decaying couch downstairs. "Where are you, Lan?"

He walked out into the hallway, unsure what to do with himself. He was exhausted, but there was no way he could sleep. So he paced. Up and down the hall, listening to the floorboards beneath his feet. They hardly creaked at all anymore. He watched as shadows played on the staircase, stretching themselves to resemble Lana's silhouette. A cruel trick of the light.

He looked away and took a deep, quivering breath. He turned his gaze toward the empty part of the hall and spotted the wallpaper hanging limp from the wall. Shawn walked to the ripped paper and lifted it up, examining the crumbled bricks beneath it.

Shawn's breath caught in his chest. He ran to Janey and Nate's rooms and banged on each of their doors. Nate rushed into the hallway from his room. He heard Janey scream, startled, from the other side of her thick oak door.

"What? What's wrong?" Janey shouted, struggling with her door before it finally opened with a loud scrape and allowed her to join them in the hall.

Shawn grabbed them both and pulled them down the hallway to the ripped wallpaper. "Look!"

"Yeah," Nate said. "No offense, man, but the place is kind of falling apart."

"No, it wasn't like that before." Shawn took a deep breath and tried to stay calm. "Lana figured out that there was a secret room behind this wall. She wanted to open it, but I convinced her it was a bad idea."

"Yeah, she told me. I told her it was a bad idea too," Janey said. "Ghosts are one thing, but a hundred-year-old walled up room is probably filled with spiders and bugs."

Shawn pointed at the torn paper and crumbled bricks beneath it. "I don't think she listened to either of us."

Shawn and Nate grabbed what tools they could find. The hammer was missing, but they found an old mallet in a cupboard and a couple of rusty screwdrivers in the laundry room drawer. Shawn dug away at the crumbling bricks with his screwdriver, while Nate used the mallet to knock away chunks of the wall.

"What if we bring the whole wall down?" he asked as two large pieces tumbled to the floor.

"Good," Shawn said, plunging the screwdriver between two bricks and prying them apart.

Janey ripped more of the wallpaper away. The bricks were laid in the shape of a large rectangle in the middle of the wall. "It's the doorway," she said as Shawn stabbed the screwdriver into another pair of bricks and wedged them away from one another until they fell to the floor.

The bricks began to give and tumble away from one another, falling a few at a time and revealing the rotting boards behind them. Those too began to crumble and fall away as Shawn and Nate struck them.

As the wall crashed down around his feet, Shawn called out for his sister. Screaming her name into the darkness, terrified of what he would find. He cried out through the clouds of dust, shouting her name, certain that she was there.

"Lana!" His voice echoed into the newly revealed room. "Lana!" He called again, his voice quivering.

The dust began to settle, and he peered through the darkness. Janey returned to his side with a flashlight. He hadn't even noticed she'd left. She handed Shawn and Nate each a flashlight, and they stepped into the room before them.

They shined their lights around the room, hoping for some sign of Lana. Shawn noticed the trunk, identical to his own, and shined the light on the wall above it. There was a large boarded up area on the wall where the missing window used to be. Shawn shivered slightly, but he wasn't sure why.

"Maybe we were wrong. Maybe she never came in here," Janey said.

Shawn looked down at the floor, and his heart sank. "She was here."

"How do you—"

Shawn pointed to the floor. There, lying on the floor, was Percival Marlow's journal. It sat undisturbed, no footprints in the dust around it. It was open to the last page.

Shawn picked up the journal. "Lana had this when I left. She was reading it to see if Marlow left any clues about the house."

"Are you sure it's the same one?" Nate asked.

Shawn reached between the pages and pulled out the letter from the curiosity shop about Mortimer. He nodded. "Yeah, this is it."

"Well, then she has to be in here somewhere. Maybe there's another secret passage or something." Janey began running around the room and pulling on the wall lamps.

Shawn looked at the last page of the journal, the page it was open to on the floor. He scanned the entries for any clue to what happened to his sister. Maybe there was something in these entries. Maybe Lana had seen something that made her come in here.

Nothing seemed especially interesting. Marlow's entries had no more talk of ghosts or whispers. But, at the end of each entry he wrote, *all remains quiet in the halls of my home*. All except the last one.

It seemed to have been added much later than the other entries; forced into the small space left at the bottom of the page. The handwriting was unsteady, like that of a much older man than the one who had begun the journal.

A terrible racket, as if the beast was breaking free of its enclosure. Boards crashing, bricks crumbling. I heard a man, his voice as clear as my own. He cried out. I made my way to the end of the hall, prepared for what I might encounter. I readied myself to come face to face with the sorrowful creature. But when I reached the source, there was only quiet. The wall was left untouched. My home returned to its pleasant silence. I considered writing nothing of it, for fear of conjuring it further. But I felt I must document this, as I had all the rest. Perhaps it was a dream. A nightmare of things past. I hope for that to be the case, but his cries still haunt my mind. His mournful, heartbreaking shouts... and the name he called out... Lana.

CHAPTER TWENTY
Back At The Shop

The book closed with a soft groan as the woman pressed the pages firmly together. She ran her hand once more across the cover and stared thoughtfully at the leather.

"Poor Lana," she sighed. "Desperate to find the ghost in her house. And, in the end, she did."

She walked to the bookcase and slid Lana's story back onto the shelf. "Shawn found the room and called out Lana's name. His voice echoed through the very soul of the house. And it spread through every wire, every wall, desperate for her to hear him. But Shawn found no one in the room. No Lana, no body... no window. He knew she'd gone looking for what lived in the walls; But then, *where was she?* It was like someone had simply removed her from the house..."

"I can't say if he ever figured out exactly what happened to his sister, but I trust that someone will. Someday." She smiled coyly. "You know, Shawn has a story of his own on this shelf." Her fingers played gently at the spine of another book. "But I think we'll save that for another time."

The shop had grown darker since she began her tale. The light from the window had faded and was barely visible at all now. The woman seemed to notice the lateness of the hour, and her eyes narrowed as she looked across the room. She furrowed her brow suspiciously, staring at the towering grandfather clock. It was now ticking faintly, its pendulum swinging in an odd, unnatural way.

"I believe our time here is done, for now," she said with a seriousness she'd not shown before.

The light from the window dwindled further into the night as she pulled the candle toward her. Wax rolled heavily down its sides. As she brought it to her lips and blew, its light shined briefly on the wooden sign hung above the counter. The name of the shop illuminated for just a moment: *The Dreary Portent.*

With a gentle puff from her pursed lips, the light vanished and all that remained were a few hazy tendrils winding upward from a faintly glowing ember. The smell of smoke from the extinguished flame drifted through the air. Darkness quickly overtook the shop.

The woman disappeared from view, vanishing noiselessly from the shop. Not a footstep, not a breath, just a constant ticking from the direction of the grandfather clock. *Tick tock tick tock tick tock*; faster and more out of rhythm. It didn't seem to care for the pacing of time at all. Soon it was practically screaming. Its haunting chimes rang out. As the ticking turned into a loud, moaning wail. A deep gong bellowed from within its wooden case.

Above the clanging and chaotic chimes of the clock came the sweet whisper of a tiny bell ringing out through the shop. A small noise that somehow muffled all other sounds. The door burst open with a breeze-less gust. The dim light of dusk shone in, lighting a path and ushering any who linger to make a hasty retreat.

Also by Megon Lashley

The Dreary Portent
The Window In The Painting
The Gold Flower Locket